# THE S.S. SHAMROCK MYSTERY

# THE TED WILFORD SERIES

# THE S.S. SHAMROCK MYSTERY

## NORVIN PALLAS

**WILDSIDE PRESS**

To Elmer and Christine.

# CHAPTER 1.

## A LADY IN DISTRESS

FOUR persons could be seen through the *Town Crier's* large plate-glass window. The most familiar of these was Mr. Dobson, the editor of Forestdale's semiweekly paper. With him were Ted Wilford, whose by-line appeared frequently over front-page stories, and his friend, Nelson Morgan, who often received credit in small type beneath the local news photos.

The fourth person was also well known in Forestdale. She was Mrs. Dundee, a former resident of the town. Ted knew vaguely that she had an interest in the newspaper, but she rarely visited the office, and he was quite certain she was wise enough not to try telling Mr. Dobson what to publish.

"Are you sure it is all right for me to borrow these young men?" she asked Mr. Dobson.

"I try to assign them where they are most needed," Mr. Dobson responded gallantly, "and your need seems the most pressing."

"What is it you want us to do, Mrs. Dundee?" asked Ted.

"I'm looking for a couple of young sailors to serve on one of my lake carriers," she explained.

"Hey, that sounds like work," Nelson protested.

"But no harder than playing football. It would be for one round trip, taking about a week, at full seaman's wages, and no preference shown you. How does that sound?"

"Not bad," Ted agreed, "but we've never had any experience on the water, you know. I suppose you have some reason for sending us besides our usefulness as seamen."

Mrs. Dundee nodded. "Yes, Ted, I do have a reason, though it might be a very silly one. I'm concerned with conditions on the *Shamrock MI.* There have been numerous petty accidents, small delays—minor matters in themselves. It's hard to tell if these are simply routine mishaps that are to be expected in any complex operation or whether there is something more behind them. Captain Weymouth has said he would like me to send someone to look into matters."

"I'm glad to know the captain feels that way," said Ted. "That will make it easier all around."

"Yes, I think it will, and I want to assure you that Captain Weymouth enjoys my complete confidence. You may feel free to say anything to him that you would say to me. As for what I expect you to accomplish, I might start with what I *don't* want. You're not spying on the men; I don't want reports on private conversations, or opinions they may hold about the company, or gripes they may have. I've found that a man who grumbles often makes a better worker than one who is indifferent to his job. There are only two things about the men which concern us: whether they are doing their work efficiently, and whether they are engaging in anything criminal. The officers watch out for the first, and I'd like you to keep your eyes open for the second."

"If we do that," Ted observed, "we may have to report suspicions—things we really can't prove."

"Yes, Ted, but if you do, I pledge my word that the information won't be used to injure anyone—unless proof is forthcoming."

"We already have a friend on the *Shamrock,* Danny Beach," Nelson reminded her. "We recommended him to you last spring."

"Yes, but I don't think that will cause any difficulty, and it may even help. You won't be able to fool Danny about why you are there, but you will have to tip him off not to tell anyone you are associated with a newspaper and know the president of Spanner Lines."

"Just how do we go about doing what we're supposed to be doing?" asked Nelson.

"Why, I'll expect you to keep your eyes open, Nelson, but even more important, your ears. It is my experience that ship scuttlebutt usually includes the truth, although you may have a difficult time sorting it out among all the rumors. And, of course, my purpose is to find out if there really is anyone who is trying to harm the *Shamrock.*"

"How many of these big freighters do you have, Mrs. Dundee?" Nelson inquired.

"We have six in operation," she explained, "and these form the backbone of our fleet. We also have one that is overage and used only on an emergency basis, and we have one being built. We are also negotiating for the purchase of another. Then, too, we have quite a number of smaller boats used for various purposes."

"All right, then, why is the *Shamrock* having all the troubles?" asked Nelson. "What about the others?"

"That is a good point, Nelson, but there may very well be a reason. The *Shamrock* is under lease to one of the large steel companies, with plants in several different cities. This contract is very important to our shipping company. I might say the Spanner Lines was one of the most respected shippers on the Great Lakes during my husband's lifetime. I was less experienced, and after his death I made many mistakes and listened to much worthless advice. Now we are getting back to full efficiency once more. It is an advantage to have a season-long contract with a steel company, and if they like our work, they may extend the contract to several more of our freighters next season. On the other hand, if they are dissatisfied they may decide not to renew our contract even for the *Shamrock.*"

"Then is it possible, Mrs. Dundee," Ted inquired, "that one of the rival shipping companies might be interested in taking over your contract?"

"Yes, I have no doubt they would like to, Ted. And there are other possibilities, too. Some of our own minority stockholders might be interested in disposing of the present company directors and getting the positions for themselves. You see, although I am the largest stockholder, I own less than half the stock. I easily maintain control because many stockholders have no interest in the affairs of the company, as long as they receive their dividend checks regularly. But if something should stir them up, they might unite against me, and I would lose control. Still another possibility is that someone has a grudge against the company or some of its personnel. Whatever the motive may be, the *Shamrock* is the best place to make trouble."

"Could you tell us a little more about the operation of your fleet?" asked Mr. Dobson, who was as interested as the boys.

"Their principal job is to bring iron ore down from the Mesabi Range in Minnesota to the steel mills on the lower lakes. Although there are steel mills on the other lakes, the principal centers are on the southern shore of Lake Erie, or the ore may be shipped inland to such centers as Youngstown and Pittsburgh."

"Isn't some ore shipped in from Labrador?"

"Yes, but that is still a much smaller operation. Since the opening of the St. Lawrence Seaway, the traffic has been growing. Even Mesabi can't go on forever."

"What do your freighters carry on the return trip?" asked Ted.

"Usually nothing. They ride in ballast. Occasionally they take on a load of coal at Toledo, but this involves a small detour and delay. Getting the ore down is the important thing. Of course if we needed a cargo badly, we could also carry down limestone or grain—provided we first washed out the holds thoroughly. Boats that alternate between coal and grain give their crews a hard time."

She smiled and apologized. "Excuse me for talking so much, but it is a subject I like to talk about."

The boys knew so little about lake shipping they hardly knew what else to ask. But they would need to be able to talk intelligently with other sailors.

"What do the letters *MI* mean?" Nelson inquired.

"They are Roman numerals. Whoever named the boat guessed that there must have been a thousand *Shamrocks* before this one, so he called it the *Shamrock One Thousand One.* I believe the crew call it *My Shamrock.*"

"Isn't it wrong to keep calling something as large as this a boat?" asked Ted. "I should think it would be a ship—not that it matters, except we don't want to sound like complete landlubbers."

"It's the custom to call *everything* on the Great Lakes a boat. Of course the crews of these big ocean ships coming up the Seaway are going to resent having them called boats."

"Do we fight 'em?" asked Nelson.

"I don't think that will be necessary," she said with a smile. "You may not even understand them, because foreign ships are making much more use of the Seaway than American ships."

She explained that her freighters did not keep to regular schedules, but raced up and down the Lakes as fast as they could. "We're never sure how much time we've got. The Soo Locks didn't open up till late April this year, and by the time winter comes in November everything's uncertain again. We always hope for a full eight months, though."

She had been notified that the *Shamrock* would be passing Detroit late the following afternoon, and it would send a boat ashore for Ted and Nelson. There would be two sailors quitting the boat at that point, so the taking on of new hands would seem perfectly logical.

"What should we take with us?" asked Ted.

"I have two duffel bags you can use. You will need a blanket and bed clothing, plus working clothes, and whatever small effects you care to take. Just ordinary working clothes will do, although most sailors like to look a bit nautical. The officers dress a little more distinctively, of course, though these are working boats."

The boys agreed to go by bus, and to travel light. Nelson, with some regret, decided to leave his press camera behind, since there would be little likelihood of getting pictures for the newspaper, and to rely on his 35-millimeter camera instead. That he would travel without any camera was unthinkable.

Having had the boys get the duffel bags from her car, Mrs. Dundee thanked them warmly as they said good-by to her and Mr. Dobson. They promised Mr. Dobson to keep in touch and left the office.

They spent the rest of the evening packing, and caught their bus in the morning.

"Ted," Nelson asked, "what do you know about boats?"

"Practically nothing. When they take the oars out and put in a motor, I'm lost."

"Well, I don't know much more. But I do know that the right side of the boat is called starboard, and the left side is port. And you don't come up to an officer and say, 'How many miles an hour are we making?' You ask, 'How many knots is she doing?' Be careful how you talk, so we'll appear to know a little bit, anyway."

"I'll try to remember," said Ted with a grin.

"One thing we can be thankful for—the *Shamrock MI* doesn't use sails. I could never get all the sails and ropes straight."

# CHAPTER 2.

## SUMMER SAILORS

THE boys were waiting on shore for the lifeboat coming from the *Shamrock,* which was anchored facing south in the Detroit River. Of the four men in the boat, two had duffel bags with them. Stepping ashore, one of the men called:

"Good luck on *My Shamrock,* boys. You may need it."

And the other added, "A four-leaf clover is supposed to be lucky, but *My Shamrock* only has three."

"And if they ever find those three sailors who were lost in the hold, let us know," the first one went on.

Nelson was assigned to a set of oars, and Ted was told to sit in the prow and watch out for small boats.

"Rowers never look around," the man in charge informed them. "You just line up your sights on two objects on shore, and row in a straight line."

They were soon at the downriver end of the *Shamrock,* and the four sailors and the lifeboat were hoisted aboard. Hardly had their feet touched the deck, it seemed, when the *Shamrock* was in motion again. They were met by Lester Custer, the boss of the deck crew.

After confirming their names he asked, "Which one of you is handiest around engines?"

There was no doubt whatever about that, and Ted indicated Nelson.

"Then you report back to the engine room, Morgan, and they'll tell you what to do. Wilford, you come with me."

"Yes," Ted agreed, uncertain how to address the man. Evidently he was not an officer, but Ted soon learned that Custer had little use for formality.

He was shown to a cabin in the forecastle, and told how to put his things away. He said he had no valuables with him, but was advised to mark his money in some way so that he could identify it.

"We have very little trouble with stealing, but with so many men coming and going, there's no use taking chances. Have you eaten?"

"Yes."

"All right, then." Custer consulted his wristwatch. "You have twenty minutes to yourself. Then report to Captain Weymouth in his quarters. He'll probably want you to fetch his mess."

After Custer left, Ted went about making up his bunk and putting the rest of his things into his locker. He had about finished when a sailor came in who introduced himself as Steve Hansen. He was about thirty years old and an old hand with no desire to become an officer, he explained.

"I've been on the Lakes for thirteen years. I'm making good money, and have a few things going for me on shore, so why should I want any more headaches?"

"Did you spend all your thirteen years with Spanner Lines?"

"No." He put his thumb behind his silver belt buckle, on which Ted saw the initials *S.H.* against a nautical design. "This is from Beatrice Lines, where I served ten years."

"How come they let you go after ten years?"

"They didn't let me go exactly. I was investigating another proposition, and waited too long to sign on."

"If it hadn't been for that you'd still be with Beatrice Lines?"

Hansen shrugged. "I'm not going to run down Spanner. Any employer who pays my salary deserves my loyalty. I'm heading for the mess hall. Want to come along?"

"I've already eaten, and I'm supposed to report to the captain in a few minutes."

"Oh, a messboy." Hansen nodded. "But you have to start someplace. Even if you're just a summer sailor, you can't tell where it will lead."

Hansen showed him how to reach the captain's quarters, and then left him. Though Ted would have liked to watch the activity on the lower Detroit River and the passing shoreline, he decided it might be best to be a little early rather than shave things too fine. He climbed the ladder to the captain's door. It was standing open, but he knocked anyway, and was told to come in.

"I'm Ted Wilford, reporting for duty, sir," he informed the man at the desk.

"Oh, yes, Ted. Glad to see you. Close the door, and sit down."

Ted did so, and the captain went on, "Mrs. Dundee told you what was wanted?"

"Yes, sir."

Captain Weymouth sat back in his chair. "Sailors are a superstitious lot, even lake sailors, and they talk. The *Shamrock* already has a reputation for being unlucky, and that doesn't do us any good. Did she explain why operations are especially critical with us this season?"

"About the contract? Yes, sir, she did."

"It's possible she didn't put it strongly enough. We need that contract badly. It may mean the difference between a successful operation and bankruptcy. Naturally it's very important to us that nothing goes wrong."

"Has anything happened so far, sir?"

"Hm—a few things, yes," the captain admitted. "There had been a number of operational mishaps, but it's hard to tell whether they were simply due to human failing, or deliberate design. We have quite a few new men aboard, and it may be that what happened came about through inexperience. I am certainly not going to accuse anyone of sabotage, unless I am very sure.

"Perhaps the thing which most disturbed me was the time we were obliged to pull in at Detroit for an inspection by immigration officials. They went through our roster thoroughly and questioned many of the men, without finding the man they were looking for. But this raises the question: why did they think he might be on our boat? Had they received some sort of tip he might be here? If so, it was a false tip, and delayed us for a day.

"Your friend, Danny Beach, is in the engine room. By all means pick up what information you can from him and the other men. It's their viewpoint we're most interested in. They may hear rumors that never reach the officers."

"What are my regular duties, sir?"

"I'm going to make you my messboy. That means you'll bring a food cart from the mess hall at each meal. I usually eat alone at my desk, which will give me a chance to talk with you regularly. The two mates off duty usually eat in their own quarters, though sometimes they join me here. The mate on duty, the quartermaster, and the radio operator if he is on duty usually take just a snack of sandwiches and coffee. Other than that, you'll be under the orders of the deck boss. Unlike the engine crew, which has to work around the clock, there are no set shifts on the deck crew. We try to do as much of the work as possible during the daytime, which gives you the evening off, but if you draw night-watch duty, then you will be given either the morning or afternoon off." He winked. "If you are supposed to be off in the daytime, I advise you to stay out of sight so someone won't put you to work."

Ted acknowledged this piece of advice with a smile and went off to fetch the food cart, heading toward the stern. Superstructures rose at the extreme ends, but other than that, the vessel had a long, level deck, expressly designed to carry ore or similar bulk freight. Long hatch covers stretching nearly from rail to rail, with a narrow path between, protected the precious ore beneath. At the halfway point a stairway led below decks, but beyond that there was nothing unusual until the after deckhouse was reached.

He found the mess hall and noticed it could seat about twenty men, half the *Shamrock's* crew. The cart was ready, with dishes steaming beneath their covers. Wondering how he was going to get it up the stairs to the deck, he was directed instead to a long tunnel which ran the length of the boat from stem to stern.

"No use letting dirt blow in on things," the steward advised him.

Ted had found the decks to be unusually clean, no doubt due to the persistent efforts of the deck crew, but knew that in dealing with a bulk product like theirs it was impossible to expect kitchen cleanliness.

He started out along the tunnel. He could not see to the end, for it followed the contours of the boat and curved outward in the middle. It was dimly lighted by a line of portholes, and these were supplemented by lights at regular intervals, which were apparently kept on constantly. In the daytime they did not help much, and at night he imagined they gave the corridor a ghostly appearance. He paused two or three times to look out the portholes. On the other side there were occasional doors leading off, but he had no opportunity to investigate them. At midpoint he saw the stairway again, leading both above and below to a lower level. There was also a gangplank, and he imagined the side of the boat could be opened up, when necessary, to let it down.

At the forward end the tunnel turned sharply, and a ramp led upward into the deckhouse. He could not take the cart upstairs, or topside as he supposed it was called, and it was necessary to carry the dishes on trays. He served the captain first, who instructed him to return when he had finished with the others. He then served the two mates in their quarters. They didn't introduce themselves or ask his name, and he realized this was the usual practice between officers and crew. He then carried coffee and sandwiches to the two men in the pilothouse. When he returned to the captain's quarters, the captain asked him to sit down again while he ate, and Ted had a chance to look around. The room was certainly nautical, with a large-scale map of the Lakes on the wall, and various decorations and instruments around that suggested maritime affairs. There was also a fine view of the water through the spacious windows.

"I hope there's nothing to Mrs. Dundee's suspicions," the captain began, "but if there is, it wouldn't be the first mystery on the Lakes, nor the last. The very first white men's voyage on the Lakes ended in an unsolved tragedy. Have you heard of LaSalle's first voyage?"

Ted shook his head.

"He built the first boat on the Lakes, I mean aside from the Indians' canoes. I don't mean Lake Ontario, of course, which is part of the St. Lawrence concourse. Anyway, he built the first boat, the *Griffin;* even had to haul it down to the river into Lake Erie by horn breeze—that means oxen pulled it. But he got it away, up through Lake Erie, Lake Huron, and Lake Michigan to Green Bay. There he traded for furs, and sent part of the crew back with the rich load. And that was the end of the *Griffin.* She was never heard from again."

"Do they know what happened to her?"

"Probably went down in a storm, either on Lake Huron or Lake Erie. As a matter of fact, some remains have recently been discovered on Manitoulin Island in northern Lake Huron—that happens to be the largest fresh-water island in the world—and it is claimed that this is what is left of the *Griffin.* I'm not too sure about it. Another story is that LaSalle's men decided to sell the furs for themselves, but were captured by Indians as they traveled overland. Anyway, they never reached any white outpost, nor could they have survived long in hostile Indian territory."

He lit a pipe and went on. "Yes, a lot of strange things have happened. Early explorers on Lake Michigan thought they were landing in China—which shows what a poor idea of geography was current at that time. LaSalle himself sailed down the Mississippi and back again, but when he tried to find the Mississippi from the Gulf end he couldn't do it. If you ever get annoyed at losing something, think of poor LaSalle and how he lost the Mississippi River!

"My own relationship to the Lakes began with a mystery, too. My father was a mate aboard the *Charles S. Price* when she went down in the Big Storm of 1913. But when his body was recovered he was wearing a lifebelt from the *Regina,* which was also lost in the storm. Fancy that." He pondered over it for a short time. "Yes, you can think of ways it might have happened, but you'll never know which is the right one, so it will always be a mystery."

"Apparently your father's death didn't discourage you from taking up the same career."

"No, it didn't. The choice was inevitable. I don't believe I ever gave serious consideration to anything else."

When the captain had finished eating, he drew some papers toward him, and Ted understood that it was time for him to leave. He began to gather up the dishes.

"Take your time, Ted," the captain advised him. "This will finish your duties for the day. We should reach home about midnight, but the deck boss will probably have duties for you tomorrow anyway. Meanwhile, if Danny Beach should be off duty this evening, he might show you around the engine room."

Ted carried the dishes downstairs, and then went for the dishes in the pilothouse, which were also ready for him. But the two off-duty mates, in their quarters, asked for more coffee and pie. It would have been easier for them to get it for themselves from the cart rather than wait for Ted, but it wasn't his place to question officers. They ate leisurely while he waited outside the door for their dishes. Then he rolled the cart back through the tunnel, now more dismal than before, and once again met no one throughout its entire length.

The mess hall was in an uproar, crowded with sailors. The mess crew did not have an easy time of things; as fast as they cleared up from one meal it was time to start the next. Even night did not free them entirely, for men coming off a late shift usually wanted a snack, which had to be ready and waiting for them to help themselves to.

Ted located Danny, who was glad to see him. He had already seen Nelson, but had had little chance to talk with him, though he understood the purpose of their mission.

"He's been assigned to the four-to-midnight shift," explained Danny, "and I've got the midnight-to-eight shift—except that I won't be working tonight. We'll be in harbor, and I'm taking off for home. I wish you and Nel could come with me."

"I don't see how we can. I've hardly started working at all, and Nel will only have one shift in. We can't expect special shore privileges already. What's Nel doing?"

"He's a wiper. He goes around with a rag and wipes off every spot of grease he can see anywhere. They keep the engine room spotless, and the floor is so clean you could almost eat off it. That's only one of his duties, of course. He has to read gauges, check valves, and act as general errand boy."

"What are your duties?"

"Same thing. John Star is the third wiper. This is his first season, too, but he signed on before I did, so he got the day shift."

When Danny heard of the captain's suggestion, he readily agreed to show Ted the engine room. Nelson was there, too, and was given permission to join them.

"You know we're powered by oil, of course," Danny began. "We burn the oil to power the steam engine, unlike the newer diesels which eliminate the need for steam. There's also such a thing as a diesel-electric, where the engine is used to generate electricity, and everything runs by electric motor."

"Is the steam engine reciprocating?" asked Nelson.

"No, turbine, rotating at about four thousand r.p.m.'s. A gear box steps that down to about a hundred. There's a smaller turbine for reversing."

He showed them a dial, something like a clock but without numbers. There were compartments for three different speeds forward, three speeds in reverse, and instructions for "stand by," "stop," and "finished with engine." At present both hands rested on "full speed ahead."

"There's one like this up on the bridge. The mate or the quartermaster sets the large hand at the proper order, and rings a bell, and back here we set the small hand to show that the order was received and is being carried out. Of course there's a telephone, too, for more complicated instructions."

They were introduced to the second engineer, Mr. Griffith, who was on duty just then, and presently the chief engineer, Mr. Owens, came in, and they were introduced to him as well. He was a pleasant man, though strictly dedicated to business.

When they had seen everything they could, and Danny had explained more to them than they could understand, Ted and Danny left the engine room. Then Danny showed Ted the storerooms, the ballast tanks, and the oil bunkers, as well as the engine crew's quarters.

"This boat reminds me of a long earthworm," Ted remarked, "who looks back and wonders if his tail really belongs to him."

"Only earthworms are blind," Danny reminded him. "But you do get the feeling of two completely different operations. The deck crew bunk in the forecastle, and we bunk back here. They come back for mess, and we go forward occasionally to visit, but other than that there's little mixing. When the captain comes back for an inspection, he always lets the chief engineer know ahead of time that he's coming, so he won't appear to be snooping. Mr. Owens is boss of steam and fuel, and doesn't like to have anyone else telling him how to do his job."

They came topside and were walking leisurely along the rail.

"Have you ever heard anything, Danny, about the *Shamrock* being an unlucky boat?" asked Ted.

Danny frowned. "It does have that reputation, though it's nothing you can put your finger on. It makes you wonder: is the management up to par, is there something slightly wrong with the boat's design, are we getting only the poorer type of help?"

"What sort of things have happened since you've been on board?" Ted inquired.

"Well, let's see. Once there was a foul-up in signals at the Soo Locks, and we missed our turn at the locks. That meant a delay of a few hours. On this very trip, going up, a lifeboat broke loose and went overboard. Ask any sailor and he'll tell you something like that should never happen on a well-run boat. A missing lifeboat means you're breaking safety regulations and asking for trouble, but this time, luckily, we were able to recover it.

"On one of my first trips it was a flu epidemic that knocked out almost half the crew. Or was it flu? Some of the men thought it was food poisoning, because it hit mostly the men at a particular mess. It didn't hit all of them, however, and it did hit a few who weren't at the mess, so you can't prove anything. Everyone recovered in a couple of days, but meanwhile we were shorthanded.

"Of course I've never had any experience on a boat other than *My Shamrock,* so I don't know whether these are commonplace things that you learn to take in stride, or whether they are very unusual. I only know how the men act. Whenever something happens, they just shrug as though to say that you expect things like this on *My Shamrock.*"

They were out in Lake Erie now, nearing the passage between Pelee Island and Pelee Point, off Southeast Shoals. The sun hung low in the sky behind them.

"Going to wait up to see the arrival in port?" asked Danny changing the subject.

"No, I think I'll turn in. I'll have a full day's work coming up tomorrow, and Nel will be tired, too."

"Then I won't be seeing you till tomorrow night. Take it easy." Danny left, having given Ted plenty of things to think about.

# CHAPTER 3.

## A CHANGE OF PLANS

WHEN Ted awakened the sun was already bright. He felt as though something was wrong, but for a few moments he was unable to think what it was. Then he realized the boat was moving, although they were supposed to be in harbor. Even if they were heading up the river to the unloading docks, they would be under tow, and he thought he could feel the throbbing of the freighter's own engine. He looked out the porthole, and saw that they were out on the lake traveling at full speed.

He looked at his wristwatch. It was seven o'clock, and he was due to get the captain's breakfast at seven-thirty. He was alone in the cabin, but by the time he was dressed Hansen came in.

"What happened?" Ted inquired.

"A change of plans. We're going on to Buffalo."

"I thought we were all ready to dock at midnight."

"We were, but just before we pulled in the order came to go on."

"Isn't this unusual?"

Hansen shrugged. "Unusual that it came so late, I suppose, but changes of orders come all the time. Some boats leave the Duluth-Superior harbor having no idea what port they are going to, but certain they will be able to get rid of their load somewhere. You see, there are no regular schedules, and if one harbor is congested, you may be able to unload and turn around faster by going to another port. You don't get paid for waiting time. The idea is to make just as many trips as you can before you get your tail frozen off."

"I understood the *Shamrock* is under lease to one of the steel companies."

"Yes, but they have a plant in Buffalo, too, and decided that was where they wanted us."

Ted remembered that Danny would be one of those most disappointed. Even though he still got his shore leave in Buffalo, it wouldn't be the same as getting home.

In the crowded mess hall Ted heard plenty of gripes about the change of orders, but a few sailors who lived around Buffalo or had friends there were glad. He brought the food cart back for the officers, but had no chance to discuss anything with the captain, who was conferring with the first mate, Kirt Bowling. This delayed matters for Ted, and it was a quarter after eight before he was able to gather up the dishes. As he did so the captain's telephone rang.

"Captain here," Captain Weymouth answered. He listened for a while, and then began to scowl. He hung up and ordered, "Forget the dishes and get Mr. Bowling here on the double."

Mr. Bowling had just left but Ted located him at the door of the deckhouse, and delivered the captain's message. The first mate immediately retraced his steps, and Ted followed. He supposed his duty was either to deliver the dishes or make himself available for further orders, but he was curious as well.

He entered the room after the mate, and though the captain noticed him, he paid no attention. His voice was sharp.

"We've apparently lost a man overboard."

"What?" The mate looked stunned. "Who was it, sir?"

"A wiper, John Star."

Ted realized this was the third wiper Danny had mentioned, and that seemed to bring it closer to home.

"When did it happen, sir?"

"'He was just missed now, when he failed to report for his eight o'clock shift. He wasn't in his quarters, and a quick check seemed to show that he was nowhere around. He was last seen around eleven o'clock last night. It could have happened at any time between then and eight o'clock."

Mr. Bowling waited for orders.

"Launch a general search. It's possible he's still on board somewhere. I want every foot of this boat searched."

"Yes, sir." The mate hurried from the room.

Ted hesitated. The captain noticed, and said:

"You may as well return the dishes. There's nothing you can do. Mr. Owens is coming forward to talk with me."

Reluctantly, Ted left the captain's quarters. By the time he had assembled all the dishes, he knew from the commotion around him that the news of the disappearance was already generally known and the captain's orders were being carried out. There were even searching parties in the tunnel, which had always been deserted during his previous trips.

He found the same stir in the after deckhouse. No one was eating quietly in the mess hall, which was only half filled. Those who were eating were talking excitedly, grabbing bites in between. Ted located Nelson, and before they had exchanged a dozen words Danny also joined them. He had been relieved from duty, though normally a man stays on duty until his relief man appears, no matter how many hours it takes. None of them had eaten, and it was decided to take some sandwiches, oranges, and bottles of milk up on deck.

"I was the one who discovered he was missing," Danny explained, as they watched the commotion on deck. Searchers were running here and there. There was no place to hide on the long deck, between the two deckhouses, except between the rows of hatch covers, and this possibility was speedily eliminated.

"How about in one of the holds?" Nelson suggested.

"How are you going to get the hatch covers off?" Danny demanded. "That takes a crane, unless you want a dozen men straining their backs."

"Well, what do you think we ought to do?"

"The best thing for us to do is stay out of the way," was Ted's advice.

Nelson caught a certain note in his voice, and asked, "Don't you like the way things are going?"

"No. Nobody knows where anybody else has searched."

"What's the difference? With thirty men milling around, they ought to find him if he's here to be found."

"Unless somebody is helping him hide."

This put a new light on things. It would be possible, they supposed, for someone to tell a group of searchers that he had already looked in a certain place.

The search continued, but the frenzy wore off, and as more and more possible places were eliminated, it became even more haphazard and finally lackadaisical. John Star hadn't been found or the search would have been called off; and it was beginning to look as though he wasn't going to be found.

"Did you know him well?" Ted asked of Danny.

"Pretty well. We palled around together when we had shore leave."

"Any chance that he might have swum to shore?"

"He would have been crazy to try it. I don't believe we came any closer than four or five miles from the breakwater. I thought we were coming into harbor, but when we headed out into the lake again I knew what must have happened, and I went to report for my regular midnight shift."

"How good a swimmer was he?" Ted questioned.

"He could swim, of course. I went swimming with him a couple of times when we had shore leave. But he really wasn't a good swimmer. He's one of those tall, lanky fellows who make pretty good basketball players, but fight the water too much. And then when you think of the cold water and the possibility of losing his way in the dark—no, I don't think it very likely he could have swum ashore."

"Isn't there a chance he could have been picked up by a fishing boat?"

"The fishing boats don't usually go out that far at night, and they usually take great pains to avoid the shipping lanes. There's not much point in arguing with a 25,000-ton freighter, even if you do happen to have the right of way. And if a fishing boat had picked him up, we would have heard by now."

"Maybe he planned ahead of time to have a fishing boat pick him up."

"That would be awfully tricky, too, Nel. What you have to remember is that we were near port, and there were a lot of people on shore watching us. You can see a lot with binoculars in the dark; they gather up the light. I feel sure if there had been a boat following us closely enough to pick up a man, it would have been noticed and reported."

Les Custer came up to them. "If you boys don't have anything to do, I can find something for you." Quite evidently he was fed up with the disorder on board, and intended to do something about it.

Ted started to follow him, but Danny said respectfully, "We're engine crew."

Custer gestured in dismissal, knowing that they had their regular shifts to serve. But Ted went along with him, and was soon busy checking ropes and other equipment. It was work that could have been done at any time, and kept the men busy for the present.

Presently the vessel pulled into Buffalo harbor and anchored. Ted wondered if the freighter would head directly up the river to unload, but it seemed that the loss of a man would have to be reported first. Captain Weymouth and Mr. Owens went ashore in a lifeboat. One of the sailors selected to row the boat was Danny, probably because of his connection with the missing wiper.

The deck crew continued somewhat aimlessly at their task. At noon the small boat had not yet returned. Ted supposed that he was still responsible for getting the food cart back to the mates, and was allowed to leave before the others. With this job completed—the mates looking glum and unresponsive—he joined Nelson in the mess hall.

They had about finished when the lifeboat returned, and Danny appeared at their table.

"Guess what!" he explained breathlessly. "We don't belong in Buffalo at all."

"What do you mean?" asked Nelson. "We're here, aren't we?"

"Yes, but there was no message ordering us to go on to Buffalo. Facilities are all tied up here, and meanwhile they're waiting for us back home."

"Who is responsible?" asked Ted.

"That's what the captain is trying to find out. Heads will roll today, boy!"

With the few minutes remaining of Ted's lunch time they lolled about on deck for a while, admiring their huge vessel and wondering about its capacity for hiding someone.

"She has the reputation of being haunted," Danny admitted, "but then, all large vessels do."

"How long is she?" Nelson inquired.

"The way the sailors say it, hang a fishing pole out from the stern and she'd be seven hundred feet."

Ted calculated rapidly. "That means from the forward deckhouse to the mess hall and back again is about a quarter of a mile. I hope they never forget the salt on my cart."

"I thought I saw something like a fishing pole hanging out the front end," Nelson observed.

"That's the steering pole. You'd find it plenty useful if you were up on the bridge and lining up your course with your compass."

Nelson looked at the covered holds. "So that's what this operation is all about. How much ore are we carrying?"

"What would you guess?"

"Five thousand tons?"

"You can multiply that by four, and you'd still be short. Of course it varies a little, depending on the lake level, and the harbor you're going to, and whether you're expecting rough weather."

"These freighters are really the queens of the Lakes, aren't they?" Ted asked. "Are there bigger freighters on the ocean?"

Danny nodded. "Yes, but we don't talk about them. Anyway, these are bigger than the freighters which come up the Seaway. Our lake freighters are built for one purpose, and they can't hope to compete. We make fun of them for being afraid of ice. They depend on year-round operation, and they can't take a chance on getting frozen up in the Lakes. Now our lake freighters prefer to winter in their home ports, but if they should get locked in at the Soo, no great harm is done. It's still better to take a chance on bringing that last load home."

"I still don't see why the ocean freighters don't make a lot more money, if they can work the year around," Nelson objected.

"Among other reasons, they wear out years faster, because of salt-water corrosion. Then, until the Seaway was open, the larger ships couldn't get in, and now that they can get in, they still aren't designed to match up with our loading and unloading equipment. And though our lake freighters are idle during the winter, ocean freighters need time out, too, for repairs and refitting."

Having been told that the captain had eaten ashore, Ted returned to his deck crew. Nelson, who was free until four o'clock, had his camera out and was planning his shots. Danny, who now expected to serve his usual midnight shift, was falling asleep on his feet, and decided he'd better do something about it. So Ted worked through the afternoon at tasks with no great urgency about them. Obviously, no one knew what was going to happen next, so it was impossible to make plans.

The men were inclined to dismiss the false orders which had come in by radio.

"An inexperienced radio man," one of them explained. "Lynn Kilbaine isn't even a licensed operator. He probably picked up a message intended for some other freighter."

This would be inexperience at its worst, Ted thought, and wondered why the *Shamrock* would depend on such an incompetent man. But the disappearance of John Star was of more concern to the crew. The general opinion after heated discussion was that he had fallen overboard and drowned.

"It isn't the new men who have the accidents," said one sailor, "because they're too cautious; and it isn't the old hands because they understand the dangers. It's the ones in between—and Star was just about right."

However, Ted remembered the preceding night had been calm, and Star had not been on duty. This made such an accident all the more inexplicable.

When Ted went aft for the food cart, he found it piled higher than usual. He was told that the captain had ordered an extra meal for a guest he had with him. Ted found the guest to be a Coast Guard lieutenant. Although he was introduced, he was not invited to stay, and left the officers to their own affairs. Nor was he further enlightened about the decisions they were making when he returned to pick up the dirty dishes.

With Nelson on duty and Danny possibly still asleep, since he had not been in the mess hall that evening, Ted was left to his own devices. Everyone seemed too restless for cards and no one seemed to be paying any attention to television.

Ted was standing with Hansen near the rail as twilight fell.

"There's Vega," said Hansen indicating a star almost directly overhead. "It's almost always the first star out, at this time of year. And there comes Arcturus, never far behind."

Ted looked toward the unbroken horizon. "I suppose the water is a wonderful place to study the skies. Do the stars help with the navigating? I've heard that the captain comes out every so often to shoot the sun or a star with his sextant."

"Not on the Lakes, Ted. Longitude and latitude calculations don't mean much here, and they don't have much use for loran, either.

They generally work from beacons and landmarks on the shore, and set their compass course from them."

"Aren't the boats often out of sight of land?"

"Oh, yes, but they simply hold to their course until they pick up their next landmark. Radio directional signals are available, too, if you need them."

"A magnetic compass isn't much use on the Lakes, is it, with all the iron ore around?"

"A gyroscope compass is more reliable, but the smaller boats don't have them, and the bigger boats usually keep a magnetic compass in reserve, just in case. It's a good idea to know how to deal with your magnetic deviations, because you never know for sure when you may need them."

Just then a sailor called out, "We've got our clearance. We're heading home."

The deck crew responsible for the anchors sprang to their task, and in a few minutes the *Shamrock* was sailing majestically, almost silently, out of the harbor, a creature of the night.

# CHAPTER 4.

## AN EVENTFUL MORNING

A SURPRISE awaited Ted and Nelson the next morning, when they learned that they were to be given shore leave. Danny, with a little better access to the shipboard grapevine, explained the reason.

"You were right, Ted. They're not satisfied with that search. They want to get as many men off the boat as possible, and then with a few trusted hands make another thorough search. That last one was pretty wild and woolly, though I have an idea it did the job."

"Isn't it possible that though the search yesterday missed John Star, he might have left since?" Nelson inquired.

"When could he have left? It was daylight all the time we were at Buffalo, and dusk was just settling as we left. Remember that the crew was at loose ends, and there were always some sailors lined up along the rail. I don't think he could have left in Buffalo harbor. On the way back we never got close to land again, and it was light when we entered harbor here. If he was on board yesterday morning, I feel pretty sure he's still here."

"But you don't really think he's here?" asked Ted.

"I'm sorry to say that I feel his body will be washed ashore during the next few days. Then we'll know what happened to him, but we may never know why."

All three boys had been told to report to a court of inquiry that afternoon at one o'clock. John Star's parents were flying in, and would be present to listen to the testimony of the witnesses. A prompt hearing was best from every angle, for a boat seemed to gain and lose a few hands every time it touched port.

Most of the officers and men were planning to have breakfast on shore. Unless they had homes nearby, Danny explained, they could be expected to head for the nearest restaurant and indulge themselves in their favorite foods. The food on shipboard was all right but plain, and sailors who spent the better part of the year on the Lakes often longed for something fancier.

Ted brought a snack to the mate remaining on duty, and was told not to wait for the dishes but to go on ashore with the others. He left with a boat from the prow, and Danny and Nelson went ashore in a boat from the stern. They met at the pier, which was used for docking small boats—nothing like the mammoth lake freighters. A small shore station was maintained there by the company, where sailors could make small purchases, check their bags, telephone, or leave messages.

Learning of this, Ted inquired if there were any messages for him there, but none had come. Danny telephoned his mother to let her know he had finally arrived. He had called her previously from Buffalo, having also made half a dozen more calls for sailors stranded on the *Shamrock.*

"She wants me to bring you home for a late breakfast," he announced, emerging from the phone booth.

Ted and Nelson had planned to get a room overnight, having brushed aside a previous invitation from Danny to spend the night with him. They didn't want to interfere with his homecoming, but they couldn't turn down an offer of a home-cooked meal. Besides, they were not due back on board the *Shamrock* until five o'clock the following afternoon, for it had been decided to use the most experienced help for the trip up the river. The captain wanted no more unnecessary delays.

Ted and Nelson left their small bags in the office, and walked up to the bus stop with Danny. The family car was not available, as Danny's father, a police officer, was working the day shift at present.

"That reminds me, I'd better give you my telephone number," Danny decided. "We're not listed in the book. Too many calls for my father—people he's never heard of calling him in the middle of the night, trying to get a traffic ticket fixed. I wonder what they think a policeman is, anyway?"

At the Beach home the visitors were introduced to Mrs. Beach and Sue, Danny's younger sister.

During breakfast Mrs. Beach recognized that Danny was less cheerful than usual, and when she inquired about it, he explained:

"We lost a man overboard, Mom."

"You did?" she exclaimed. "Was he a friend of yours?"

"Sort of. His name was John Star, and he was another wiper. This was his first season on the Lakes, too, so for one reason and another we often hung around together."

"How did the accident happen?" asked Mrs. Beach, while Sue listened intently, her eyes wide.

"Nobody knows," and Danny went on to tell of his discovery that Star was missing and of the subsequent search. He also told of the phony message which changed their destination to Buffalo.

"If that fake radio message came from shore," Ted said, "that means someone on shore must be connected with whatever doings are occurring on the *Shamrock.*"

"Two strange things happened the same night," Nelson pointed out, "the fake orders and the disappearance of John Star. I wonder if they could be connected? Maybe there was some reason why Star felt he had to be here that night, and when the boat suddenly went sailing past the harbor, he took a chance and jumped overboard."

"Maybe," said Danny.

"Poor John Star," Sue exclaimed. "I hope they find him," and the others echoed her wish but with much less expectation.

When the meal was finished, Danny explained that he had a few jobs to do and some telephone calls to make.

"If you don't want to just sit around, you could walk down to the park. We're less than a mile from the beach. I could meet you there in about an hour and a half."

Ted and Nelson readily agreed. It was a flawless day at the lake front. Tiny whitecaps raced endlessly toward the beach, while the blue of the water melted into the bluer blue of the sky on a distant horizon. Gulls soared on rising currents of air and spiraled above them.

Nelson snapped several pictures, but was not satisfied.

"There's no way to get it all in. I wish I had a telephoto lens to catch those gulls."

They passed the tennis courts and stopped for a little while to watch a small-fry baseball game which was being bitterly contested. But the lake was the chief attraction. There were numerous small fishing boats out, while other fishermen draped their lines from the breakwater, some of them seemingly in hope that no fish would come along to disturb their repose.

The boys decided to walk out along the breakwater, and made their way over the rough rocks, taking care not to disturb any of the fishermen. Far out near the end, an elderly fisherman sat by himself. A rowboat was tied nearby. As they approached he looked up and smiled, and seemed disposed to talk. They sat down next to him, laying aside the coats they had been carrying.

"Having good luck?" asked Nelson, uncertain whether the few fish he saw flopping in the pail would be considered a good haul.

"Good enough. We try to get what the lampreys don't."

"Having a lot of trouble with lampreys?"

"It's come danged near to killing off commercial fishing. But if our science fellows can take us to the moon, they ought to be able to lick this problem. At one time Lake Erie supplied half the world's fresh-water fish; the shallow beds made good breeding ground. You don't see many lake trout anymore. But you still get sheepshead, yellow pike, bass, carp, catfish, dogfish—"

"Isn't the dogfish a kind of shark?" asked Nelson.

"Not the kind that lives in the lake. It's a small thing with flippers like paws, and even barks like a dog. Haven't really seen one for years, though."

"We're visitors here," Ted informed him.

"That so? Then you might enjoy looking through the glasses at that freighter out there. It's one of the Pittsburgh Steamship fleet—you can tell by the way the smokestack is painted—and probably the *Arthur M. Anderson;* I noticed in the morning paper it arrived yesterday."

Ted followed the slow progress of the freighter—which bore a close resemblance to the *Shamrock*—across the horizon for a few minutes, then handed the binoculars on to Nelson.

"Notice she's riding in ballast?" asked the old-timer.

"How can you tell?" Nelson returned.

"Because she's riding high. See the difference in the color of the paint?"

Nelson shifted the glasses to other objects, finally coming to stop on a small structure miles out in the lake.

"Is that a lighthouse out there?"

"Not really. It's one of the old-fashioned water cribs, serving as an intake to bring offshore water into the city. The more modern intakes are below the surface. What do you think that black thing is sticking up?"

"Well, blow me down, it looks like a windmill."

"That's exactly what it is. Before they automated, there were always two or three men living out there during the navigation season, and that windmill charged their batteries."

"What's the matter with regular electricity?"

"They've tried that, but when they laid a cable across the lake floor, the boats kept dragging their anchors across it, and every time it happened it meant a new cable. The windmill makes out all right, even though it only gives about forty volts. And then there's a generator, too, in case the batteries fail. It's important to keep those navigation lights on all the time."

Nelson handed the binoculars to Ted, who took his turn scanning things of interest. The old-timer's attention was momentarily attracted by his bobbing line, and Nelson watched with anticipation.

"I could tell you something interesting about that crib," the fisherman remarked, having landed his squirming fish. "It happened—"

He was interrupted by a sharp exclamation from Ted:

"What's that out there?"

The fishing was immediately forgotten as the fisherman exclaimed:

"A boat's on fire, and they won't have any extinguishers, either." He made a quick size-up of the two boys, noted Nelson's firm muscles and Ted's long legs, and came to an instant decision.

"You," pointing to Nelson, "get into the rowboat with me and handle the oars. You run and get help. We'll need it fast."

Without waiting to argue, Ted scrambled over the breakwater rocks. The fire in the distant rowboat was attracting attention, but no power boat seemed available. Having reached shore he ran toward the nearest boathouse, and approached a young man who was just leaving the building.

"Rowboat on fire. They need help."

The young man wasted no words, but ran to his nearby speedboat.

"Get in," he ordered Ted, who jumped in alongside him. He started the engines and took off with less warm up than was customary.

As the nose of the speedboat swung around, Ted saw that there were three men bobbing in the water. The rowboat had flared up so quickly and the flames spread so fast that they had abandoned it, not even able to use one end of it to hang on to. But the boat with Nelson and the fisherman was almost to them, and did in fact reach then before the speedboat had attained full speed.

The young man slowed down as they approached the scene of the accident, so that his waves would not swamp the other boat or the men in the water. As they drifted in, Ted saw that Nelson had gripped one of the victims beneath the shoulder, while the others were struggling to get a life jacket adjusted on him.

"Get him over here," the young man ordered, and everyone thought this was best. Since the speedboat could not come too close through fear of crushing the victim between the two boats, Nelson relinquished his grip, and the two swimmers helped the victim to the edge of the speedboat. Then Ted and the speedboat pilot were able to lift him in to the deck. One of the other men also climbed in, and the speedboat spun about for shore.

"Bill's a pretty good swimmer," the fisherman explained, "but he must have hit his head on something. Did you ever pour fuel into a hot outboard motor? Make sure you never do. The whole thing flared up before we knew what happened."

A crowd had gathered by the time they reached the pier.

"Fire engine's on the way," someone volunteered, and Ted was glad someone had had the sense to do something. The victim was breathing heavily, semi-conscious.

They lifted him ashore and tried to empty the water from his lungs. The firemen arrived soon after, and took charge. They soon had the victim standing on his feet.

"I feel fine," he said groggily, swaying.

"Well, we'll take you along to the hospital anyway for a checkup," and he was too dazed to refuse. His friends followed along in their own car, after expressing their thanks to everyone who had helped.

The crowd gradually dispersed. Ted and Nelson returned to the breakwater for their coats, and said good-by to the fisherman, who said he was leaving that day for Arizona.

Danny arrived on schedule, and was told of the rescue.

"Hadn't we better be getting to the bus stop?" Ted suggested.

"Oh, there's a quicker way to get downtown than that," Danny explained.

"By boat?"

"Yes, a speedboat. I usually arrange to rent it from a friend of mine when I'm home. I phoned him a while ago, and he said I could have it."

He turned toward the same pier where Ted had run for help. They reached the same boathouse, and it was the same young man who stepped out to meet them. He was introduced as Frank Steinway, and they shook hands laughingly, as though they had just met.

Arrangements were quickly completed, and the three boys set out. Nelson was particularly interested in the mechanical aspects of the boat, and asked many questions, while Ted was content to feel the spanking breeze ruffle his hair and keep his eyes alert to everything that was going on around them. They were not greatly rushed for time, and Danny settled down to a pleasant cruising speed, even circling occasionally to give them a better view of points of interest.

At one time he remarked, "I hope we're not disturbing the men working down under us."

"Skin divers?" asked Nelson, peering into the cloudy water.

"No, even lower than that. Can you guess?"

His guests could not, and he went on to explain, "Salt mines—long tunnels reaching out from shore."

"I sure hope their roof doesn't leak," was Nelson's comment.

As the *Shamrock* came into view, Danny slowed the boat down almost to an idle, allowing his passengers to study the vessel at a fairly close range.

"But not too close," he said with a laugh. "The deck watch is touchy about strange boats coming too close, and I don't want anybody to get the idea that I'm trying to smuggle John Star ashore."

"Are the ocean freighters built along the same plan as these lake carriers?" Ted inquired.

"Not quite. Because of the large ocean waves breaking over the prow, the forward deckhouse has to be set back a little. You might say the same for the stern, too: because of the need for greater stability the engine has to be moved farther forward. But don't get any idea the Lakes are tame. The ocean waves sweep you along, while on the Lakes the waves are shorter, choppier; but you can still chop down a tree with short strokes of an ax. Lake Erie can be especially treacherous because it is so shallow a storm can churn up the bottom and set off a real ruckus. That's what you'd expect anyway, from the name."

"Wasn't it named for a tribe of Indians?" Ted questioned.

"Yes, the 'People of the Cats.' But of course they weren't speaking of our domesticated kind. 'Lake Wildcat' would probably be a good translation. Strangely enough, Erie was the last of the Great Lakes to be discovered by palefaces. Niagara Falls discouraged exploration by water, and the Iroquois Indians discouraged exploration by land."

As always Nelson had his camera with him, but lamented his inability to get decent pictures from the unsteady speedboat.

"Anyway, how could you get it all in and show any detail?" asked Ted. "I'll bet when the bridge calls the engine room, they have to pay long-distance rates."

Nelson shook his head. "I wish I could. It would make a fine picture against the green water."

"Green?" Ted protested. "It's blue."

"Green," Nelson insisted.

Danny knew better than to take sides in an argument between friends, but he offered, "Call it what you want to, but I'll say this: Lake Superior is a good deal bluer. It's colder and deeper and clearer—maybe that's why the lampreys don't like it."

They were circling the *Shamrock* very slowly and at some distance.

"She looks the same from the port and starboard sides," Nelson remarked. "How many knots does she make?"

Danny looked at Ted, puzzled. "What's the matter with him?"

"Oh, he's just trying to make like a sailor."

"Why, did I say something wrong?" asked Nelson.

"Not exactly, except that they're getting to say 'right' and 'left' instead of 'starboard' and 'port,' and the word 'knots' isn't used much on the lakes. The speed is usually given in miles per hour."

"Well, I'm glad I tried it on you first," Nelson remarked, but whatever he intended to add was stifled by a cry from Ted:

"Hey, Danny, isn't she adrift?"

"Oh, don't pay any attention to that. She always tugs a little at her anchors." He turned to look at the *Shamrock,* then suddenly exclaimed, "You're right, she *is* drifting." He gunned the motor until he was in quite close, then turned it off and shouted through his hands. "Ahoy, *Shamrock!* You're drifting!"

The motion, so slight, had not yet been observed aboard, but the cry stirred the watch into action. The boys saw men scuttling about and soon whatever adjustment was necessary had been made.

"What happened?" asked Nelson.

"Probably the stern anchor cable slipped. The bow anchor keeps the boat from swaying, but probably wouldn't be enough to hold it. More heads will roll when Captain Weymouth hears about this."

"Maybe no one will tell him."

"It's the duty of the deck watch to report anything of this kind. But that wouldn't matter. I think Captain Weymouth would know it if anybody moved his precious boat a single inch. He's a real old-time salt—a fresh-water salt, I mean."

"Was there any real danger?" asked Ted.

"Probably not. The deck watch would have noticed it before things got very far out of hand. Still, it's just one more thing."

# CHAPTER 5.

## COURT OF INQUIRY

THOUGH they were in plenty of time, the hearing room was well filled when they arrived. Captain Weymouth came in soon afterward. Even if there had been no braid on the cap which he held carefully in his lap, it would not have been difficult to guess that he was an officer of some sort on the Lakes. There was an easy-going competence about him that inspired trust, even though he occasionally fidgeted with his cap, as though land affairs were annoying to him and he was eager to get back to his vessel.

Most of the crew were present. The Coast Guard was represented, as was also the harbor master, whom Danny pointed out to his friends, but the actual questioning was conducted by an attorney with a special knowledge of maritime affairs. The first witness called was Captain Weymouth, perhaps more because of his rank than because of any personal knowledge he had of the matter under scrutiny.

Upon being asked, he stated that he had been asleep at the time the change of orders had been received.

"The mate on duty had orders to awaken me when we arrived at harbor."

"When the change of orders arrived, was not this a sufficiently important matter for the mate to wake you?"

"That would be entirely a matter for his judgment."

"Do you have any fault to find with his judgment as he exercised it?"

"Sir, if I do, it will be a matter I will discuss with him in privacy, and not in a public hearing of this nature."

"Then as a matter of fact you were not aroused during that entire night?"

"That is correct, sir. I awakened myself during the night and inquired about matters, then returned to sleep."

"Were you personally acquainted with John Star?"

"I knew the young man by sight. He was one of the engineering crew, so he did not personally come under my jurisdiction."

"At what time were you informed of his disappearance?"

"At shortly after eight o'clock in the morning. I understood that a perfunctory search had failed to find him, and I therefore authorized a general search of the entire vessel."

"With no results?"

"None whatever."

"Were you satisfied with this search?"

"No, I was not. It seemed to me to be altogether too haphazard, confused. For that reason I ordered another search this morning, after most of the crew had gone ashore."

"What were the results of this search?"

"The same—negative."

"Then you are satisfied that John Star is not on the vessel?"

"That is my opinion, sir."

"And that he probably was not on the vessel at the time of the first search, either?"

"That is the probability, yes."

The attorney glanced at the other members of the examining board. "Any more questions?" He seemed to be including not only them, but anyone else in the room. He even looked across at a troubled couple whom Ted now realized were the parents of the missing sailor. Mr. Star shook his head slightly, and Captain Weymouth was dismissed from the witness chair.

The first mate, Kirt Bowling, was then summoned. He testified to receiving the faked orders.

"You were at the radio yourself at that time?"

"No, I was not. The radio operator was Lynn Kilbane."

"A licensed operator?"

"No, sir. That is not necessary, as long as he is working under a licensed operator. All the mates are licensed. Messages are so few that we do not require the services of a full-time radio man—which, of course, would mean three men for the three shifts. As we approached harbor, I turned the radio over to Kilbane, and gave my full attention to the direction of the vessel."

"You had no reason to question the authenticity of the message?"

"None whatever."

"Would not prudence suggest that you radio for a verification?"

"If I had had any reason to doubt the message, then that is what I would have done."

"The message appeared to be perfectly regular in every way?"

"Yes, sir."

"You can say that, even though you were already considerably south of a straight line between Pelee Island and Buffalo? You had now suffered a substantial detour. Did you not find this strange?"

"It was inconvenient, but not strange. I am a ship's officer, not an officer in the company, and I carry out my orders to the best of my ability. If the company thought a change of destination desirable, even at that late time, then it was my duty to comply with the orders."

"Do I understand, Mr. Bowling, that your reaction to the orders was then to change course so as to reach Buffalo by the most direct route?"

The first mate hesitated. "That would be very near to the truth. But the fact is that we were so close to harbor, where many of the crew had friends and acquaintances awaiting them on shore, that I saw no harm in continuing for a short time as though we were to enter the harbor there. Then when the watchers on shore saw the *Shamrock MI* sailing past, they would be aware of a change of destination, and would not be put to the inconvenience of waiting futilely for many additional hours."

"You yourself had such a friend awaiting on shore?"

Mr. Bowling flushed. "Sir, I do not consider that a proper question."

"Then I withdraw it. This additional detour which you authorized was only for a few miles?"

"Yes, sir. Had a much greater distance been involved, I should certainly never have done such a thing."

"How close to the entrance of the harbor did your vessel come?"

"No closer than about four miles, I would judge. I felt that that was sufficiently close for the observers on shore to identify the vessel."

"Did you, at any later time en route to Buffalo, approach the shore any closer than this?"

"During the period that I was in charge, no. We were much farther out. I would assume the same to be true of the succeeding watches, but I am not competent to testify to this."

"Then if the missing man, John Star, were to attempt to swim to shore, the best opportunity for him would be at the time you approached within four miles of the harbor?"

"That would be a matter of speculation."

"What was the normal time for you to be in charge of the bridge?"

"From four o'clock to eight o'clock, both morning and evening. We followed the customary practice of four hours on and eight hours off, around the clock."

"In that case, why were you on duty between eight and twelve o'clock that evening?"

"The second mate complained of a migraine headache coming on. I therefore offered to spell him on his trick. It is a courtesy to exchange shifts with another person when there is a valid reason for doing so."

"Then you had been on duty for four hours that morning, and for nearly eight hours that evening—in other words, for nearly twelve hours out of the last twenty-four. Did you not feel the pressure of these excessive hours?"

"I was not unusually fatigued. I felt perfectly competent to carry out my duties. The second mate's headaches were usually of short duration, and I had every reason to believe that he would be recovered by the next day and stand his regular duty, and possibly even relieve me from part of mine."

"You did not consider the second mate's illness to constitute an emergency?"

"I did not, sir."

"Had his illness continued, then you would have reported the matter to the captain?"

"Yes, sir. In such a circumstance the captain himself frequently serves a trick on the bridge. But under the existing circumstances I did not feel obligated to inform the captain in advance of the change in plans."

"Were you acquainted with John Star?"

"I knew him slightly, and may have exchanged a few casual remarks with him on occasion. But the officers on the bridge have very little to do with the engine crew."

"During the hours of your duty, did any incident occur which might help shed any light on the matter under examination?"

"To the best of my knowledge, there was no incident of any sort. Except for the false orders, my trick was purely routine."

There were no further questions, and Mr. Bowling was dismissed. Then Lynn Kilbane was called to the stand. After being sworn in and identified, he answered questions as to his radio experience. Although he was not yet licensed, he seemed to be competent. He said that he was studying to become a ship's officer, which would include all necessary radio training.

The examiner continued: "Let us try to pin down the source of this message which you received. Did you believe it to originate in the customary commercial channels?"

"No, sir, I did not."

"Then where did you think it originated?"

"The company also has its own radio service. As Mr. Bowling has explained, messages are not frequent, and whenever anything important arises, the commercial channels can be utilized. The company service is more informal, I might say chatty. It is not particularly powerful, so the range is quite limited. If atmospheric conditions are just right, you might be able to pick up a message as far away as the upper lakes, but it wouldn't be anything to rely on. For efficient service the company would have to build several relay stations around the lakes, and keep them manned around the clock. Our business does not justify it."

"Then just what is the purpose of this company radio?"

"It is used principally to talk to vessels down in the harbor or up the river, or vessels passing the harbor. It could also be used for vessels some distance farther up or farther down the lake. Crew members often call in personal messages for their families or friends who might inquire at the office about them."

"Was the message you received identified as coming from the company radio?"

"It was."

This was all Kilbane was able to report on matters. Mr. Banner, a company officer, was then called to the stand. He was asked if the company radio had been manned that night.

"No, sir, it was not."

"Would you normally man it when a vessel was expected into harbor?"

"We would, yes, in daylight. After office hours it would be manned only if there were some urgent reason for doing so. I knew of no such urgency that night."

"Could the company radio have been used that evening by some unauthorized person?"

Mr. Banner thought very carefully before replying. "If you are asking for my opinion, I would say that the company radio was probably not used. It is locked up in a separate office, and there were no indications that the equipment had been disturbed. But if you are asking me about possibilities, I would have to admit that such a possibility exists. The outer office, and the radio room itself, were both locked. But we have never worried particularly about burglaries, since we have an excellent safe and an excellent alarm system, and we are not accustomed to keeping substantial sums of money there. Keys to both the office and the radio room have at various times been made available to various persons, and there no doubt have been opportunities for duplicate keys to be made."

"Which persons could have access to the keys?"

Mr. Banner shook his head. "I could not possibly attempt to answer such a question. I simply don't know. This has been going on over a period of years, and personnel is always changing. It could happen that a key is possessed by a person no longer in the employ of the company."

"Such a possibility did not lead you to change the locks?"

"Sir, the necessity for such a step never seemed apparent, until this incident arose."

With no further questions suggested by anyone, Mr. Banner was dismissed, and Danny was called to the stand. The first questions asked of him concerned the circumstances under which he had discovered Star was missing. He related how he had gone to the cabin in the early morning and found Star gone and his bed made up.

"The fact that his bunk was made would not necessarily prove that it was not slept in, would it?"

"Well, no. I suppose he could have slept in it for a while, and then made it when he got up."

"As a matter of fact, isn't it a habit for sailors to make their bunks when they get up?"

"I suppose it is, for many of them, at least."

"But assuming it had not been slept in, was there any other place where he might have slept?"

"On warm nights we often get permission to sleep up on deck. But in that case a man would take his bedding along with him."

"This night in question was not particularly warm?"

"No, just moderate. As far as I know, no one slept on deck that night. But occasionally a man who finds the cabin stuffy will go out on deck for a little while, hoping to be able to sleep when he gets back."

"How many bunks were there in Star's cabin?"

"There were three."

"One of them was yours?"

"Yes, sir. But I was on duty that night, from midnight till eight o'clock."

"What about the hours before midnight? Do you know whether Star had retired?"

"No, sir, I can't say. I was in the cabin very little that evening, for I prefer to sleep after getting off duty. Our particular cabin is not square, for the funnel runs through one corner. Star's bunk was out of sight around the corner."

"What steps did you take when you discovered Star was not in his bunk?"

"I inquired of some of the other fellows if they had seen him. No one had, so I reported to Mr. Owens, the chief engineer. He got several of us together with orders to look more carefully. We did so, with no further results, after which a general search was instituted."

"Were all of Star's effects still in the cabin?"

"As far as I could tell, everything was still there except what he would ordinarily be wearing."

"How well did you know John Star?"

"I didn't know him at all before we both signed up on the *Shamrock*. But he was a wiper, too, and I suppose that was one of the things that helped to draw us together."

"Had he ever spoken to you about any personal problems?"

Danny considered. "I shouldn't like to put it that way. When you're thrown together a lot, you can hardly help talking about yourself a little. We both speculated some about the future."

"Did he have any problems of health or money?"

"As far as I know his health was good enough, except that he seemed to have trouble hearing. He was waiting a call into the Army, and meanwhile he had joined the summer sailors. He had his draft papers moved here, and every time he reached port he inquired about it."

"Were you acquainted with his swimming ability?"

"Yes, I was." Danny frowned. "I wouldn't say he was any great swimmer, though he seemed to enjoy it."

"Is it possible that he had more swimming ability than he displayed to you?"

"On the contrary, I felt that he was showing off a little, pretending to be better than he really was."

"Then do you believe he could have swum the four miles from the freighter to the breakwater?"

"It is my opinion that he could not, nor even as much as a single mile."

"Even if he had been wearing a life jacket?"

Danny looked momentarily startled. "Well, I hadn't thought about that. But it was dark and the water was cold, and even with a life jacket you have to be able to propel yourself through the water. It isn't only drowning that you have to worry about. Exposure and exhaustion can get you, too."

"Did you talk with Star during the day before he was lost? What was his mood?"

"He seemed to be in a normal frame of mind, as far as I can recall. Of course he always was a little bit moody."

"Did he convey any hint to you that he was thinking of abandoning the *Shamrock MI*?"

"No, nothing of that sort."

"Was he close enough to you to tell you of his personal plans?"

Danny thought it over and finally said, "That would be very hard to say."

The attorney looked around, and Mr. Star rose to his feet. "Is it true that my son suffered a shipboard accident—a blow on the head?"

Danny had to stop and think. "Oh, yes, I remember now, but that was weeks ago. It hurt for a while, but he shook it off. He assured everyone it wasn't anything."

"Did he ever complain of dizziness or headache after that?"

"Not to me, no, sir."

"Did he ever miss duty due to illness?"

"He was down with flu one time, but so were a great many others. That's the only time I know about."

"Thank you," and Mr. Star sat down again.

Danny's testimony had brought an odd feeling to Ted. There was a question he wanted to ask Danny, but was unable to do so just then, as the next witness was called. This was the chief engineer, Mr. Owens. He verified Danny's story of how he had been notified of John Star's disappearance, and the subsequent search.

"How adequate do you feel that your search was?"

"That first general search? We did the best that we could."

"How many persons participated in the search?"

"Why, nearly everyone on board, I guess, except for those whose duties required them to maintain their posts."

"Since the search failed to find him, are you prepared to swear that he was not on board?"

Mr. Owens shook his head. "Mr. Attorney, if you were ever on an ore boat, you would understand that no one could swear to such a thing."

"And the search this morning was even more thorough?"

"I suppose that it was. I did not participate in it."

"You consider it possible that John Star might be on the *Shamrock MI* at this very moment?"

The engineer gestured helplessly. "It is possible, but very unlikely."

"What sort of activities might have led Star to fall overboard accidentally?"

"Since he was not on duty, I can only imagine horseplay or extreme carelessness. But if it were horseplay, probably a number of other sailors would know about it, and I feel sure that at least one of them would be honorable enough to report it."

"What do you think of the possibility that he left the vessel voluntarily?"

"I can see no point to it. He could have left at any port he pleased."

"Then what is your opinion as to his disappearance?"

"I can only see it as an act of violence or desperation."

A hush fell over the courtroom, but the attorney did not pursue the topic. His next questions took a different tack.

"If a sailor had certain valuables in his possession, might he ask to have them locked in the ship's safe?"

"Yes, sir, he could do that."

"Did John Star ever make such a request?"

"He did not."

"You don't know of any valuables in his possession?"

"I was not aware of any."

The attorney looked at his notes before asking, "Were there any life jackets missing that morning?"

So far the engineer had been giving his answers in a calm and deliberate manner, but now he seemed befuddled. "Not officially, sir."

"I'm not sure I understand that answer, Mr. Owens."

"Well, the number of life jackets checked out all right. But there were a number of discarded life jackets lying around that were not included in the official count. These were old or damaged in some way. It's possible a man could have repaired one for himself. Or it's possible that they were thrown out."

"There's no way for you to tell if one of these old jackets was missing?"

"No, there was never any check made on them, I tell you."

An annoyed tone crept into the engineer's voice.

"These discarded jackets were sub-standard?"

"Obviously they did not meet our safety standards, or they would not have been discarded. But as everyone knows, the perfect life jacket hasn't been invented. It's a question of displacement and buoyancy. A plump person needs less help from a life jacket than does a slender person, and a child needs even more."

"If John Star attempted to swim to shore, do you think he would want a life jacket?"

"It's a question what you expect of a life jacket, whether you want it to hold you up till you get picked up, or whether you are trying to get somewhere. A confident swimmer would prefer not to have a life jacket holding him both up and back."

"Did you ever have occasion to criticize Star's work?"

"No more so than any other novice's. These men aren't children, and they know how to follow orders."

"But he did make some blunders?"

"Nothing more than usual. Nothing worth mentioning."

"Isn't it true that the more experienced men try to make things tough for the newcomers?"

"There is a normal amount of teasing and nicknaming and fool's errands, and the like. This is customary hazing procedure."

"Did John Star show any resentment at this hazing procedure?"

"Not that I was ever aware of. Actually it's a kind of compliment. At least somebody realizes you're *there*. After a while the kidding stops, and you feel you belong."

"You were not aware of any personal problems Star might have been facing?"

"I was not, sir."

The attorney looked around, but no one seemed to have anything further to offer, and Mr. Owens was dismissed. Other witnesses followed. The third mate testified that, upon taking over the bridge at midnight, he returned the vessel to its normal route, though at an angle, so that it did not approach any closer to land. Other shipmates of the unlucky sailor testified as to what they knew about his personality, but no one knew him as well as Danny did, nor had much to offer.

The attorney faced the spectators. "Is there anyone else who has any information to offer this court?" No one spoke up, and he then requested a recess of fifteen minutes, apparently for the purpose of consulting with Mr. Star.

Now Ted had a chance to ask his question of Danny. "If he was on the *Shamrock* all season, something must have delayed his Army call. Did he ever tell you what it was?"

Danny looked doubtful. "He never said anything like that to me. Where are you going, Ted?"

"To make a telephone call. I'll be right back."

It took Ted a little while to find a telephone, and a little longer to wait for it to be available, and several calls and much tact to get the information he wanted. When he returned to the hearing room, Mr. Star was being interrogated.

"Was John's home life satisfactory?"

"We tried to make it so. Young men always have their problems, but his seemed no worse than normal."

"His health was good?"

"It was, unless that bump on the head affected him more than we know. He spoke of it jokingly in a letter home."

Ted wrote on a note:

"John Star was disqualified for Army service," and passed it to a court attendant to give to Captain Weymouth. The captain read it, and handed it to an assistant, who carried it up to the attorney. He read it, then asked the witness:

"Did you know that your son had failed to qualify for military service?"

"Nonsense." Mr. Star's manner was brisk. "I refuse to believe it. His hearing wasn't that bad."

The attorney turned about. "Where did this note come from?" Ted stood up. "Where did you get your information?"

"I telephoned the Army about their standards, and then the draft board. They referred me to his personal physician."

The attorney returned to the witness. "Do you still question this information?"

Mr. Star hesitated. "Well—it may be true, but it doesn't prove anything. He probably wanted a summer on the Lakes before returning home and settling down to the family hardware business. He always had a notion about being a sailor, but it's something he would have outgrown."

A different tone seemed to have entered into the hearing. Until now the assumption was an involuntary accident. Now there was a stronger feeling that Star himself was responsible. Further questions were asked of the father, but he had nothing more to contribute. It was announced that the court would release its finding within a few days, and the hearing adjourned.

"Unless the body is found," Danny told his friends, "they won't be able to come to any definite conclusions. Your observation put the damper on that, Ted. How did you happen to think of it?"

"Well, if he liked boats why didn't he try to get into the Navy? Probably because the standards are stricter—and that made me wonder if he could qualify even for the Army."

"Four miles—even in a life jacket?" asked Nelson. "Could he do it, Danny?"

"It would be taking a chance, and why should he do it when he could have jumped ship in Buffalo?"

"You know what I think?" Nelson went on. "I think he doesn't get along at all with his parents, especially his father, and that he doesn't want to enter the family business."

"All I can say," Danny offered, "is that if John Star is alive, but is letting his parents think he's dead, he ranks pretty far down in the scale of animal life."

"Well, everybody can't be as lucky as we are," Ted observed. "When is the last time you had an argument with your father, Nel?"

"The time I crumpled the fender on the family car, and told my father that was the reason I ought to have my own car. He didn't think that was a very logical argument, but I won out finally."

Captain Weymouth had been busy talking with several men, but now started down the aisle that would take him past the three boys. Noticing Ted, he seemed to give him a slight nod of approval, then walked on toward the door.

"I admit I'm getting more confused by the minute," Nelson confessed as they, too, left the courtroom and headed down toward the pier. "Where does all this talk leave us?"

It was left to Danny, the most experienced of the three, to try to answer.

"I think we can almost rule out any ordinary kind of accident. Nel, you spoke about the possibility Star had to get ashore that night, so he tried to swim. Mr. Owens suggested the possibility of foul play. Ted has shown that Star wasn't going into the Army. And maybe I can add my own bit to all this, though it isn't the sort of thing I could testify to in court. I do kind of get the feeling, now, that Star was up to something all along that I didn't know about. It's hard to pin it down, because nobody tells everybody everything about himself, and some people are naturally more reserved than others. But I do think he had some plan in mind."

"Then where do you think he is now?" Nelson demanded.

"I think," said Danny soberly, "that he tried to swim to shore and didn't make it. You see, it's really a lot more than four miles. If he were to come straight to shore someone might see him and report him. He would have had to take a long detour around. I just don't believe he could do it."

"And you don't think a boat picked him up?" asked Ted.

"No, not a chance near the harbor, nor afterward, when disappointed sailors were lining the rails. And there wasn't much chance before. One of the sailors did report seeing him around eleven o'clock."

"That fake radio message has to be a plot, doesn't it?"

"It certainly sounds like it, though the way nearly everything manages to get snarled up sometime it might be an honest mistake. Maybe someone pulled a booboo and doesn't want to come forward and admit it." Danny shook his head slowly. "But a fake message would have to sound so much like the real thing. The sender would have to know what kind of orders we had already received, and it would have to sound so innocent that the first mate wouldn't be likely to ask for a verification. I'd say it's more likely to be a plot than a mistake."

# CHAPTER 6.

## NIGHT IN THE HARBOR

AT the pier they met Mr. Keats, the second mate. Apparently he had been relieved by Mr. Bowling, after the first mate gave his testimony, and was on his way to the hearing.

"Is it over already?" he asked. "Then I guess they didn't need my testimony after all. Anyway, there's nothing I could have told them."

"How's the headache?" asked Danny.

"Oh, it was practically over that night. I could have served my regular shift, but Mr. Bowling thought I'd better not."

"That was kind of him," Ted offered.

"Kind? I supppose so." Mr. Keats grinned. "But I figured he was mostly interested in working up some extra shore leave for himself, and who am I to argue with a superior officer?"

"That isn't quite the way Mr. Bowling told the story on the stand," Nelson recollected after the mate left. "He more or less said Mr. Keats asked to be relieved."

"They could both be telling the truth the way it looked to them," Ted pointed out.

It was Danny's intention to return the speedboat to its owner, and then to spend the night at home.

"I've got extra leave time coming. You can usually trade someone—two hours of work at sea is worth one hour of shore leave. That's pretty high interest, but it's the going rate."

"Do they need the engine crew while they're in harbor?" asked Nelson. "I thought we wouldn't use power on the river."

"We don't, but steam has to be maintained every minute, from the time the season starts until it ends. As far as the engine crew is concerned, if we can give the bridge all the steam it needs from first to last, then it's a successful season for us—even if the company loses a million dollars."

Ted obviously had something on his mind.

"In case I wanted to see Captain Weymouth, what would be the best time and place?"

"I imagine he'll sleep aboard the boat tonight. You can always ask at the company dock. They'll know if he's ashore or not. And if he's on *My Shamrock,* you try to hitch a ride out, and hope to see him. Good luck!" Danny did not sound particularly hopeful.

"You know what's on his mind, don't you, Danny?" Nelson put in. "He thinks he's going to find out what happened to John Star. And the only way that'll ever be solved is that either they'll find the body, or else they'll find him. But Star is either in the lake or else he's hundreds of miles away by now. Let's see you pull *that* rabbit out of a hat, my good friend."

"What's the schedule on the *Shamrock?* " asked Ted. "Will they tow her up the river today?"

"I doubt it. It's pretty late in the day, and I don't believe they care to work on her after dark. Besides which, these tugboat captains are a touchy bunch, anyway. I imagine she'll be going up first thing in the morning, and we'll still be able to clear port by late tomorrow. Thank goodness there's no objection to running at night on the open lakes."

"The *Shamrock* won't have to wait in port for the report on the inquiry, will she?"

"There's no reason why she should. All the testimony is in. The verdict won't change anything."

They were not in any particular hurry, though hunger pangs were beginning to stir. Danny invited them to take a little spin, but they declined. After he had taken off, having promised to call them in the morning, they got themselves something to eat and then Ted tried to call Mr. Dobson, but it was after ten before Ted could reach him. He told him about the new developments on board the *Shamrock.* Everything he had to say was news to the editor, although it was possible Mrs. Dundee had already had a report on matters.

"I think it's important to get in touch with her, Ted. She's traveling on company business, so I'm unable to reach her right now, though I will in the morning. Meanwhile, I think there's one important thing to be done. If there's a possibility of a leak at the company office, then I think it better for Captain Weymouth to report directly to Mrs. Dundee, rather than through the office as usual. Do you think you could get him to agree to that?"

"I believe so, Mr. Dobson. I'll tell him tonight, if I'm able to see him on the *Shamrock*. Will you have Mrs. Dundee call me, then?"

"I'll give her your information, Ted, and if she has further instructions for you she'll call you before nine. Otherwise carry on as usual."

When Ted told Nelson of his intention to go out to the *Shamrock* that night, he offered to go along, but Ted declined.

"I don't want it to look like too big a thing. Besides, you can help by being here in case Mrs. Dundee calls. I can't reach her, but she may try to reach me."

The lakeside station seemed to be open all night, at least when one of the company's vessels was in harbor, and Ted inquired inside whether the captain was on board. He was told he was, and was further given the loan of a rowboat in which to reach the vessel.

"Here's a flashlight to take along, in case any boats approach too close. And there's a life jacket under the seat. If you can't swim, put it on."

Ted thanked him, and shoved off in the rowboat for the *Shamrock,* with both the life jacket and the flashlight at his fingertips. Nervously, he felt obliged to look out for other possible small boats, for the harbor was very black in that long stretch between the shore lights and the *Shamrock.* As he approached, he could see a ladder hanging from the stern, so he headed in that direction.

He tied up, using a knot which he felt sure would hold, and scrambled up the ladder. He was immediately challenged by the deck watch, but identified himself, and was allowed to pass without being required to state his business. It occurred to him that he ought to stop in the mess hall for some sandwiches to take to the captain, which would give an ostensible reason for his errand forward—and he took an extra sandwich for himself, munching it as he hurried forward.

Captain Weymouth was in his quarters, and accepted the sandwiches absent-mindedly. Then he listened to Ted's suggestion concerning the reports.

"Did this order come directly from Mrs. Dundee?"

"No, it was from Mr. Dobson. He intends to call her in the morning."

The captain nodded, knowing of the close relationship between Mr. Dobson and Mrs. Dundee.

"I'll do that, Ted. It was a question in my mind just how much I must necessarily tell the home office."

Whatever his suspicions were regarding that unauthorized radio message, he wasn't going to tell Ted anything, and Ted had nothing to report other than speculations it would be useless to discuss. One point bothered Ted, however.

"I don't think it was brought out in court, but who was in charge of the search which was made this morning?"

"Mr. Griffith, the second engineer." His tone asked the unspoken question, "Why?"

"Well, it just occurred to me that no search would be any good if one or more of the persons doing it were determined to hide something."

"Mr. Griffith is a top-flight man," the captain assured him, "and he handpicked a small group of trustworthy men. I've known Mr. Griffith for many years, and when you really know a man, he can no more change his character than he can change his fingerprints. I'm sure he feels the same about the men he chose."

As far as the captain was concerned, this seemed to close the matter, and in the absence of any facts to the contrary, Ted was obliged to accept Captain Weymouth's judgment. The trouble with a situation like this was that it made you suspect everybody.

Taking his leave of the captain, Ted went down the stairway to the main deck. Then he walked back along the rail toward the stern, choosing the side which faced out on the lake. The lake was dark and impenetrable, and, far out at some un-discernible boundary, lake and sky blended into a common blackness.

The deckhouses fore and aft were brightly lighted, but their brightness only dimly penetrated the center of the boat. Ted passed a half-dozen hatch covers hiding the precious ore beneath. He was not particularly jumpy, but the strangeness of his surroundings gave him an eerie feeling as he recalled that it was on just such a night, perhaps somewhere along this same rail, for this was the darkest portion of the deck, that John Star had disappeared. Thoughts of this led him to quicken his pace, and he soon passed the midway point and began to approach the brightly lighted stern.

A sound of something from the water caught his ear, and he leaned over the rail. This was the side of the boat which was sheltered from the harbor lights, and at first he could see nothing. Then he caught sight of a small boat—a motorboat, although its engine seemed to be turned off or extremely quiet. Closer and closer it drifted in, silently, as though avoiding the lights of stem and stern. What might have happened he was not to know, for suddenly the operator of the motorboat took alarm. He gunned his engine, swung about, and rapidly faded into the night. Only by chance, as it passed the lights of the stern, did Ted see the name painted on the rear. It was the *Gray Lady.*

The name meant nothing to him, but the behavior of the boat was puzzling. Had it been attempting some kind of rendezvous with someone on board the *Shamrock?* That seemed to be the only reasonable explanation. Ted looked about him, closely studying the deck for any trace of movement. He saw nothing, although the deck was covered with shadows. Stillness surrounded him, except for the *Shamrock* tugging at her chains and the gentle lapping of the water against her sides.

What ought he to do—investigate, report the matter? It seemed that only his own untimely and unexpected presence there interfered with the completion of whatever scheme was afoot. Was it any of his business? He decided not to investigate. Prudence told him that if there was indeed someone there on deck with him, that person might be better prepared than he was to commit some act of violence in order to avoid discovery. And anyway, he might be dreaming up the whole thing. He didn't see anyone; he had no proof that the *Gray Lady* was seeking to establish a contact with anyone there, nor that the purpose was necessarily nefarious. The operator might simply have been anxious to get a closer look at the freighter. Or perhaps he had a friend on board with whom he wanted to talk.

Still, the motorboat hadn't shown any lights, and had left abruptly at a speed greater than that permitted in the harbor. Ted remembered having seen an item in the paper that evening about after-dark water skiers in the harbor—which was equally a violation of the laws. He hadn't seen any skiers, but there may have been some, and if that was all the motorboat was up to, it wasn't up to him to enforce the law.

At the stern ladder he referred the matter to the watch.

"Did you hear a motorboat go by a few minutes ago?"

"Seems to me I did, but I didn't pay much mind. You expect it in harbor."

"He seemed to be drifting toward the *Shamrock* without power, and then suddenly gunned up and sped away. Maybe it was because he saw me, I don't know."

"Well, I'll send another man up to watch to make sure he doesn't try it again. If he rams us we might be delayed for repairs, or worse yet if he breaks his fool neck we might be tied up here for days while they try to blame it on us. I don't suppose you saw the name."

"Yes, I was able to catch it as it sped away. It was the *Gray Lady.*"

"The *Gray Lady?*" The watchman laughed. "All right, let it go. I'll report you saw a motorboat coming too close. Never mind the name."

Ted was unable to figure out why the name should seem either humorous or incredible, but he awaited the return of the watchman.

"Want a lift ashore?" the watchman inquired.

"No, thanks, that's my rowboat."

"There's a boatload taking off in a minute. You might as well ride with them. They can tow the rowboat."

Several crew members soon made their appearance, and agreed to take Ted ashore. As they prepared to lower a lifeboat, the watchman remarked:

"This hand claims he just saw the *Gray Lady.*"

"Yeah?" The sailor in charge didn't seem much interested. "He's not the first one."

Another sailor looked at Ted more closely. "Say, this is the captain's new messboy. Probably doesn't have the sod shook off his shoes yet. Maybe he doesn't know about the *Gray Lady.*"

"What about her?" asked Ted curiously.

"Well," the watchman explained, "what if you told me the name of the man piloting her was John Smith, what would I think?"

"Well—that might really be his name."

"Sure, but it might also mean that you didn't know his name, or you weren't going to tell me, or maybe you never saw him at all. That's the way sailors feel about the *Gray Lady.*"

"Aren't there really any boats named the *Gray Lady?*"

"Sure, probably lots of them, just as there are thousands of men named John Smith. But that doesn't change matters any."

"Maybe he never saw a boat at all," a sailor suggested.

"No, I heard the motor myself," the watchman returned.

"Then it can't be a ghost. Ghosts don't make noise."

"The devil they don't," another sailor objected. "My aunt had one in her attic and—"

"Stow it!" ordered the man in charge. "You can yarn all you want to on shore, but why waste time?" He studied the rowboat below. "You tie the knot in that line?"

"Yes," Ted admitted. "It isn't loose, is it?"

"Loose! It looks tight enough for a tow-line. Well, maybe I can get it out."

They all got into the lifeboat, which was lowered into the water, and the crewman did manage to free the rowboat with the aid of certain muttered incantations. Then they stroked for the shore.

# CHAPTER 7.

## UP A RIVER

AT the breakfast table Ted related to Nelson the story of his nocturnal adventure.

"Whatever the *Gray Lady* was up to, I think I prevented it—provided the watchman really did send a man up on guard."

"And if he was reliable," Nelson finished. "When you start getting suspicious, where do you draw the line?"

"But what could he have been planning? I'm certain he intended to come right up next to the *Shamrock.*"

"You know how some guys are when they get behind a motor." Nelson shrugged, inclined to dismiss it. "I'm sure somebody got a kick out of buzzing the *Shamrock,* just the way some student pilots get a kick out of flying too low." But his second thought was more startling. "Hey, Ted, you know something? He may have been trying to smuggle John Star off the boat!"

It was an exciting idea, but Ted put the damper on it. "Except that everybody agrees that John Star isn't on the *Shamrock.*"

"Yes." Nelson's voice was still raised. "That's what they all say, but nobody's sure."

"The boat's not too far out in the harbor now," said Ted, willing to pursue the subject but without much belief. "Don't you think he could swim ashore if he wanted to?"

"Maybe not—and there's the problem of wet clothes when he is ashore. That's the very thing that would attract attention to him, and maybe he can't afford it."

With nothing better to do, they discussed the matter further, all the time awaiting Mrs. Dundee's call. When it did not come by nine o'clock, Ted felt that he was free to continue as before, confident of Mrs. Dundee's approval.

"Or she may have run out of gas somewhere far from a telephone," Nelson suggested, and laughed as Ted scowled.

Then Ted was summoned to the phone, but the caller was Danny.

"How'd you like to go up the river today and watch *My Shamrock* unload?"

"That sounds good to me. Do we ride on the *Shamrock?*"

"No, she's left already. I'll be by in the speedboat and pick you up at the company pier in half an hour."

On board the speedboat, Ted related to Danny his adventure with the *Gray Lady.*

"There must be something fishy going on out there," Nelson pointed out.

"We haven't been able to prove very much," Ted cautioned him. "The loose lifeboat and all the other things Danny told us about could have been accidents. And John Star could accidentally have fallen over the rail, no matter how calm a night it was."

"He did have that bump on the head," Danny recollected.

"What about the radio message, Ted?" asked Nelson. "But, of course, that came from shore, not from the *Shamrock.* Where do you think that message came from, Danny? I don't think it was the company office."

"I figure it had to be the company office, because nobody else could know enough about what was going on. Don't you agree, Ted?"

Ted frowned in what Nelson often called his "thinking scowl." "I can see three possible answers: the company office, some other transmitter, or—no message at all."

"Huh!" his friends exclaimed.

"Well, how do we know for sure there ever was a message? Lynn Kilbane could have faked it."

Nelson groaned. "How many more men are we going to suspect? Is even Danny on your list?"

"Right at the top," said Ted with a grin. "He pushed John Star overboard because he wanted to work the day shift instead."

No more was said about the *Gray Lady.* Perhaps, after all, the best explanation was that it was the work of somebody out for kicks. Ted found it much easier to dismiss the matter in the bright sunshine than it had been last night on the gloomy midsection of the *Shamrock* surrounded by dark water.

Danny had turned up the river, and they followed its meandering course, under huge bridges and through the city's industrial complex. They passed smaller bridges, too many to count, which they were able to go under, but which would have had to be lifted to permit the passage of the big freighters, delaying traffic all along the way.

They could easily see now why the freighters had to be towed up the river. They could never have maneuvered around those curves under their own power. Though ordinarily there was room for two freighters to pass each other in opposite directions, they had better not attempt it on the bends.

The boys felt it remarkable that the river, so narrow, would be deep enough to accommodate such big boats, and Danny informed them that it was dredged constantly to a depth of twenty to twenty-five feet.

"And then the silt is dumped just outside the harbor. That's one of the causes of the lake's pollution."

After seeing more than they could absorb, or even ask intelligent questions about, the visitors spotted the *Shamrock* up ahead, some huge steel structures hovering over her.

"Those are the Huletts. They're for unloading the ore, and they can do a whiz job. Either the boats were made to match the machinery, or the machinery was made to match the boats, and they're a pretty efficient pair."

"Don't they use electromagnets to unload the ore?"

"Say, what do you think ore is like, anyway?"

"I—I don't know," said Nelson lamely. "I thought it was something like hard chunks of rock."

"Well, it isn't. It's little pellets of red earth, though the color and texture vary with different kinds. But they do use electromagnets for scrap iron."

For a while they watched the machinery scooping the ore out of the holds, while they calculated how long it would take if it had to be done by men working with hand shovels. Supposing that one man could shovel twenty tons a day, it would take a thousand days for one man, or about a year for three men, to get just the one freighter unloaded; the machinery would do it in a few hours, with very few men in attendance.

Then they rode on a little way farther up the river, passing the turning basin, but Danny did not want to go too far. The river was not dredged above the steel mills, and though it was deep enough for their small boat, the debris was not cleared away, and he didn't want to snag on something, particularly in a borrowed boat.

So they turned around, and started leisurely downstream. In good time they reached the lake again, and Danny invited them to come home with him for lunch.

Accepting gratefully, the visitors remained in the boat as it turned toward the suburbs. At the pier they were met by Frank Steinway, who inquired about their trip.

"Say, Frank," Danny asked of him, "did you ever hear of a boat called the *Gray Lady?*"

Frank's eyebrows shot up. "There are probably lots of them. If you want information—real or yarns—I can tell you where to get it. Take a run up to Resthaven Cove, where there's a home for retired sailors. You'll get all the yarns you want. And while you're up there, you might look up my friend Captain Blair. He can give you the real dope about almost anything going on on the Lakes. It would make a nice afternoon's jaunt."

Danny shook his head regretfully. "We haven't time. *My Shamrock* is sailing this evening."

"You sure about that?" asked Frank quizzically.

"What do you mean?"

"Didn't you hear about the strike?"

"What strike?"

"Tugboat strike. Didn't you have your radio on? The news flash just came over." He laughed. "Well, don't look so shocked over it. I thought it would be good news for you—give you a little vacation."

But of course it wasn't good news as far as Ted and Nelson were concerned. What did this do to their assignment on the *Shamrock?* And Danny, too—though he might enjoy a few days at home—was trying to earn all the money he could during the summer. If his money ran out during the coming school year, it wouldn't be funny. Ted thought of this, and asked him:

"Does this mean we're laid off?"

"No, not right away, I don't suppose. We'll be on the payroll until we're notified that we're not. But it does put the company in a spot.

They've either got to pay the men or lay them off. One way they might be paying them for weeks or a month for doing nothing. The other way they lay them off, the strike is settled, and they're all ready to sail—but no crew available."

Ted exchanged glances with Nelson. Could this be one more of those things that seemed to be happening to the hapless *Shamrock* with regularity? It was hard to see how any one individual could have started a tugboat strike, but possibly it could happen.

"What's going to happen to the *Shamrock?*" Nelson inquired.

"She's up a river, isn't she?" said Danny bitterly. "And that's where she's going to stay for a while. As far as *My Shamrock* is concerned, the strike couldn't have come at a worse time."

"How come? The tugs took her up the river. Doesn't that mean they're obliged to take her down again?"

"Don't count on it. A wildcat strike means that discipline has broken down, and anything goes. We'd have been a lot better off if we'd waited around at Buffalo—or even if we were out in the harbor now with a full load. We could get out of the harbor by ourselves and head for some other port. Up a river is about the worst place to be in time of trouble."

"If it's only a wildcat strike, maybe it will be settled quickly," Ted suggested.

"Maybe, but you can't count on it. Sometimes those things keep spreading, and the union might come around to authorizing it, if it thinks the men have a solid grievance."

"Why do these things have to happen during the busiest part of the season?" Nelson demanded. "Why can't they get all these things settled during the winter, when they've got plenty of time to sit down and talk, with nobody hot under the collar?"

"Man, that's not the way the world's run," Frank offered. "Who'd even know they were on strike during the winter? When you decide to fight, you want it to hurt."

"Only they might end up getting clobbered worse themselves."

"There's always that chance. I guess if everybody knew how a fight was going to come out, there wouldn't be very much fighting going on in the world."

Danny looked at his companions. "Well, then, Frank, maybe we will rent your boat this afternoon, if we can. You fellows want to?"

Nelson said a quick, "Yes," and Ted added, "This time the trip is on us," to which Danny agreed.

"How well do you know Captain Blair?" he asked Frank in parting.

"Well enough so that he tries to sell me his boat every year. The *White Rover* is a real buy, but I can't swing it. Tell him it's a deal, if he'll take trading stamps!"

At the Beach home, Danny's mother greeted them as though they were expected, then said to her son:

"There was a telephone message for you. I was out at the time, but Sue took it. Did you hear about the strike?"

"Yes, we did, Mom."

The three boys went into the dining room, where Sue was busy setting the table.

"Hi, Sue. Who called me?" Danny inquired.

"Grant."

"Grant?" He puzzled over it for a moment. "I don't know anybody named Grant. Was that his first or his last name?"

"He didn't say. He just said, 'This is Grant.' You know, like General Grant. Look, I wrote it down in shorthand." She reached for her notes.

"Are you sure his name wasn't Lee? Maybe he was a Southerner."

"No, it was Grant. Mother," she called, and Mrs. Beach came to the doorway. Sue showed her a symbol on the paper. "Isn't that Grant?"

"Yes, it is, dear. Don't let him tease you." "Well, what did Grant say?" asked Danny with artificial patience.

"He said he'd see you. I thought you'd know all about it. I tried to get it all down in shorthand, but he talked too fast."

"Look, Sue," said Danny in exasperation, "why didn't you just listen to what he had to say instead of taking it down in shorthand?"

"I have to practice my shorthand this summer, don't I?" she exclaimed defensively.

As the boys went on into the living room, Ted remarked, "I understood you had an unlisted phone, so strangers couldn't call you."

"We do, but you know how your number can get around. This Grant sounds as though he knows me. I wonder what he wanted?"

"If it's important, he'll call back," Nelson decided.

"No, it sounds like he gave the message to Sue. But I agree it couldn't be anything very personal, or he would have waited for me."

The television set was switched on to the news. The wildcat strike was prominently played up, and the boys learned that the *Shamrock* might unwittingly have played a part in touching it off. The issue seemed to be whether the tugs should pick up the boats outside the harbor, or whether they should be allowed into the harbor under their own power, as the *Shamrock* had done.

"What do you think about it?" Nelson asked Danny.

"It's a ticklish proposition. Of course these big boats can't maneuver. As long as they're coming straight in, or making a wide turn—and there isn't room for much of that in the harbor—they're all right."

"Any danger of their running aground?" asked Ted.

"No, the harbor is dredged deep enough, I believe, but they might run into something. The more congested the harbor, the more danger there is. They're under much better control with tugs. The bigger boats don't try to dock themselves, though I suppose they could if they had to. But why take foolish risks with a boat worth millions of dollars?"

"I suppose there's not much danger, as long as they run slowly and take everything easy," Nelson observed.

"No, Nelson, you've got exactly the wrong idea about that. It's the stream of water flowing past the rudder that makes the boat maneuverable, so the slower the boat is moving the poorer control the quartermaster has over it. Haven't you ever wondered why the rudder is on the back end of the boat? That's because a greater stream of water is created there. What would you think of a boat that had a rudder on the front?"

"I'd think the designer made a mistake."

"It's done occasionally, for a boat like an ice-breaker that has to do a great deal of backing up. Otherwise the control is poor on a boat that's reversing."

"Then just what is the objection to having the boats towed into the harbor?" Ted inquired.

"The double fee. If the freighters could go right up the river, it would be one thing, but usually they have to wait their turn. So they pay to get towed into the harbor, and pay again when they go up the river. They don't think the first tow is necessary. My guess is that most of them would prefer to anchor outside the harbor—provided the weather wasn't bad."

As the news broadcast continued, it seemed evident that the issue of giving the tugboats all the business within the harbor on the large boats was the principal point at stake; and there also seemed to be some difference of opinion on just what a "large" boat was, though it had to be larger than a tugboat, or who would tow the tugs? Efforts were being made to negotiate the issue, but it appeared that little progress had been made.

"Anyway, we can have a nice afternoon," Danny decided.

# CHAPTER 8.

## RESTHAVEN COVE

AS they cruised along, Danny gave Nelson a chance to get the feel of the tiller. Ted kept his eyes on the map and attempted to chart a course to their destination, as well as keeping his eye on everything around him that seemed of interest. Whether they ever would have found Resthaven Cove by means of Ted's chart was debatable, but Danny recognized some of the landmarks as they approached, and they were soon ashore. The first person they met proved to be the captain himself.

"What can I do for you?" he asked.

This question was not easily answered, but Danny made the attempt.

"We really came out for the ride, but Frank Steinway has been telling us about your boat, and if we had a chance to look it over, that would be something. If you could tell us something about the *Gray Lady,* that would be interesting, too."

Captain Blair snorted. "If you want to hear about the *Gray Lady,* go on up to the old sailors' retirement home. But my *White Rover* is something else again. You boys aren't in the market by any chance, are you?"

"Not for a while yet," said Danny. "We're still in college, though we're working on the *Shamrock MI* this summer."

"Well, I don't mind a chance to show my boat off to you. Tell you what, I'll do even better than that. I'll take you for a little spin, but I've got a little tinkering to do with the engine first. Why don't you go up to the home for half an hour, and then come back for a ride? They've got a nice little museum up there, and a telescope in a tower, through which they claim they can see Perry's Monument at Put-in-Bay. I've never been able to see it myself, but that's what they claim."

"Are visitors welcome?" asked Ted.x

"Oh, yes, they're always looking for someone whose ear they can bend. Don't let them take advantage of you. But take your time. If you're not back in half an hour I'll wait."

"Do you know of any boat named the *Gray Lady?*" asked Ted as they started to leave.

"Yes, it happens I do. At least I heard of a motorship named the *Gray Lady* and owned by somebody named Joseph Hunt, a Canadian. I've never seen it, nor have I met Captain Hunt."

"I thought I saw a motorboat named the *Gray Lady* prowling around the *Shamrock* in harbor last night."

"If it was, I don't think it could have been Hunt's. I heard that he's cruising the inland waterways along the Atlantic this summer. Some fellows seem to have all the luck, and the rest of us have to work for a living. I take out fishing parties during the summer, but in the winter I have to work ashore."

"You're not sure if Captain Hunt has left Lake Erie?" Ted persisted.

Captain Blair shrugged. "He didn't confide his plans to me. I can only report what I hear."

The boys left him then and started up the beach. There was little to see in the town, but upon inquiry they were directed to a long hill a short distance outside town, on top of which sat the mariners' home. Steep though the hill was, they didn't mind the climb, though they could see that it might be difficult for aging limbs. But the view from the top of the hill easily explained why that particular site had been chosen. They could see over the tops of the trees that lined the beach, and had a beautiful panoramic view of the lake itself. The water seemed to dance and sing in the sparkling sun. They could see boats out there, too, and imagined that they were not far from the major shipping lanes. So these retired mariners never totally lost contact with the water they loved.

There was a flag fluttering from a very high pole, and this was probably one of their chief prides. Several men, sitting in lawn chairs and enjoying the weather, spoke to them as though they were old friends. A sign directed them to the office, and there they met Captain Murphy, who seemed to be in charge of the home. He was a retired seaman himself, but still active and alert.

"Welcome aboard," he said traditionally. "Do you know anyone here?" When they said they did not, he went on, "Then I imagine you came to visit our museum. Right this way, gentlemen."

He led the way to an adjoining room, where they found the walls covered with maps and prints, many shelves of books, and display cases filled with strange exhibits. Captain Murphy explained some of these things to them, but was presently called away by a bell, and they were left to wander among the exhibits themselves. These were probably of little commercial value, though they represented a lot of work and sentiment on the part of the men who had gathered them.

It would have been interesting to spend hours in that room, with someone to spin the yarns that attached to many of the objects, but they had neither the time nor the guide at present. It would be something to return to, sometime in the future.

Returning to the office, Ted inquired of Captain Murphy, still busy at the desk, "Is it true that you have a telescope here with which we can see Perry's Monument?"

"It's true we have a telescope," said the captain, smilingly refusing to comment on whether the monument could be seen or not, this apparently being an institutional joke. "Why don't you try it for yourselves? Take the elevator to the fourth floor. Captain Xerxes is up there now, and he'll help you."

When they were out of earshot in the elevator, Nelson remarked, "Seems as though everybody who ever stepped foot in a boat is a captain. When do we get our degrees?"

"After you retire, the way they did," said Danny, chuckling.

Captain Xerxes greeted them with casual warmth, and directed them in the use of the telescope. They each had a turn, and each had to confess that he was unable to see Perry's Monument.

"I'm afraid there is a slight haze today," the new captain apologized, and the visitors wondered if there would always be a convenient haze.

Just the same, they all took another turn, and enjoyed picking out the boats on the lake and some of their occupants. Everyone was aware of that telescope on the hill, and one fellow even seemed to be waving at them.

"Have you ever seen the *Gray Lady?*" asked Ted.

"Oh, yes, many times," said the captain. "She is a frequent visitor to Resthaven Cove."

The visitors tried hard not to look startled at this piece of intelligence. But whom were they to believe, Captain Blair or Captain Xerxes? Ted tried to pursue the subject without seeming particularly interested.

"Would that be Captain Hunt's *Gray Lady?*"

"I'd hardly be in a position to know that. You must draw your own conclusions." He looked at Ted more closely. "Haven't I seen you here before with Captain Blair?"

"No, this is my first visit here."

The captain shrugged. "Then it must have been someone else. Though I could have sworn it was you. Used to be pretty good at remembering faces, but my memory isn't what it used to be, and besides it *was* several weeks ago."

They thanked him for his help and courtesy, but he turned down a donation, saying that cash was never accepted, but surplus household articles would be cheerfully welcomed.

"Better luck next time," he called as they parted, but they were rather disinclined to share his optimism about the monument.

"You know what I think?" said Nelson, after they had thanked Captain Murphy and left the building. "I wouldn't believe anything that any sailor ever said to me. They don't know where truth leaves off and fancy begins. You know why he claimed the *Gray Lady* was a frequent visitor here? Because he didn't want to spoil any good story we may have heard."

"That could be," Danny agreed. "That's why he wouldn't tell us which *Gray Lady* he thought it was, though he must have an idea about that, if she really did come in here. It's just a pleasant story to him."

He brooded for a moment. "You know something funny? Captain Xerxes thought he saw Ted before. Well, Ted and John Star are really built much alike. They could be mistaken for each other from a distance."

"What would John Star be doing here?" Nelson demanded. "Anyway, if that was weeks ago, it wouldn't have anything to do with his disappearance."

"I know—it was just an idea, and maybe not a very good one."

They were late getting back to Captain Blair, but he did not seem impatient. Apparently he had used the interval to spruce himself up, and possibly his boat as well.

"All ready for our spin?" he asked. They agreed and hopped in, and he shoved off. Turning was not a difficult problem with him, for he had twin propellers.

"That's what *My Shamrock* ought to have," Danny exclaimed.

Captain Blair seemed to enjoy both their pleasure and their questions. He went on to explain many technical features about the *White Rover,* in which he seemed to take much pride. When a lull developed, he asked Ted:

"Is the *White Rover* very much like the *Gray Lady* you saw last night?"

"Why," said Ted thoughtfully, "it seems to me the *Gray Lady* was a little larger, and she had a carrier over the cabin, and the exhaust pipe was different. I only got a little glimpse of her in the dark."

His friends, relying on him to take the lead, were waiting to see if he was going to relate what Captain Xerxes had said to them. Ted saw no reason to keep it secret, and was interested in getting Captain Blair's reaction.

"A captain up at the home said that the *Gray Lady* came in here quite often."

Captain Blair grunted disdainfully. "What do they know? They seldom come down to the beach any more. Just remember that those old fellows are all wool and a yarn wide."

"I wonder why they made up a story like that?"

"What else are they supposed to do with their time? I'll tell you what I'll do: if a motorboat named the *Gray Lady* comes into this cove today before you leave, I'll let you have the *White Rover* for two weeks, rent free and all the motor fuel you need."

This was a very generous offer, but Captain Blair seemed so sure of himself that they felt they had little chance to collect on it. They studied all passing boats with close attention, but by the time they were drawing up to the pier again admitted themselves defeated.

"And we could have used a motorboat for two weeks," Nelson lamented, "with this tugboat strike on."

"How can you be sure that Captain Hunt's *Gray Lady* might not just happen to show up here this afternoon?" asked Ted.

"Because Hunt isn't even on the Lakes, and if he was, why should he use this cove? He never has before."

"Then you're still sure it wasn't Hunt's boat I saw last night?"

"I'm not sure about the boat. It could have been his, from the little bit you were able to describe it. But I do know Captain Hunt wouldn't behave like that. He's a wealthy sportsman, not an irresponsible kid."

He chuckled to himself as he thought of something. "You know how Hunt's boat got her name? He wanted to call her the *Lady Grey,* but the sign painter made a mistake. So he decided to let it stand."

They tried to thank Captain Blair, but he waved their thanks aside. "I didn't have a job for this afternoon. Call it goodwill and advertising. If you ever want to get a fishing party together, you'll know where to find me."

"What about the lampreys?" Nelson called above the noise of the engine which Danny had started.

"Forget the lampreys. I know places even they haven't found."

Then they took off, waving till they had cleared the cove.

# CHAPTER 9.

## ANCHORS AWEIGH

WHAT do you think of Captain Blair?" asked Ted. "A blow-off," Nelson decided. "He thinks he's smarter than the lampreys."

"Well, what's he supposed to say?" Ted responded. " 'Please hire me as a fishing guide, but don't expect to catch much because the lampreys have everything.' He wouldn't get much business that way."

"Maybe the lake pollution will kill the lampreys," Danny suggested, "and then everything can start over. What did we really accomplish on this trip, Ted?"

"We found out that either the *Gray Lady* visits Resthaven Cove or else she doesn't. Which story are we supposed to believe?"

"Neither one," said Nelson. "Sailors are all alike—present company excepted."

"I don't see how we can disbelieve both stories," said Danny with a good-natured laugh. "But I thought Captain Xerxes was sort of rambling, while Captain Blair was very sure of himself. At least he was pretty sure the *Gray Lady* wasn't going to show up today."

Ted grew thoughtful. "Maybe that's the story, Danny—*today*. He knew the *Gray Lady* wasn't going to show up today—why? Maybe because he knew the only *Gray Lady* around here was elsewhere? He claims he thought that, but also said he wasn't too sure about it. Could it be he knew because he warned her to stay away?"

"Warned her? How, Ted?" asked Nelson.

"Maybe with a radio message. You noticed he didn't ask us on the *White Rover* right away. In fact he seemed anxious to get rid of us for a while. He said he had some tinkering with the engine to do, but how do you fellows look after you've been fooling around with an engine?"

"Pretty greasy," said Danny, and Nelson agreed, adding:

"And it doesn't come right off, either."

'That's right. We weren't gone too long, but when we got back he was all spruced up. I don't think he'd have had time to play around much with the engine and get rid of all traces of oil in the little while we were gone. So, maybe all he did was send a radio message."

"But we're overlooking the fact that Captain Blair is a friend of Frank's," Nelson suggested.

"Just because he's trying to sell Frank a boat doesn't make them buddy-buddies."

"The *White Rover* is a pretty good boat, isn't it? Why is he so anxious to get rid of it?"

"I can see you're not a boatman," said Danny, laughing. "They're always dreaming about something better. Some fellows won't be happy till they get the *Queen Mary.*"

"Well, what do you think of the *Gray Lady* Ted saw?"

Danny thought it over. "Undoubtedly Ted saw a boat called the *Gray Lady,* but I still think the best explanation is some sort of joke. The name wouldn't necessarily have to be painted on the boat. A little cardboard hung in back would be good enough in the dark."

Remembering how spooked he had felt while standing on the darkened *Shamrock,* possibly close to the spot where John Star had disappeared, Ted felt it hard to believe it was intended as a joke. At least Star's disappearance was no joke.

"What would be the chances of keeping a boat hidden?" Ted inquired.

"Something like *My Shamrock,* there'd be no chance at all. Now a small boat would be altogether different. There are thousands of places to hide her—in some secret cove, say, or up a river."

"There's an even simpler way to hide a small boat," Nelson reasoned. "Just paint her over and give her a new name."

"That's true enough. Small boats are always popping up out of nowhere. Of course you'd have to do a little fancy work to get her a new registration number, or doctor her up with an old one."

They had their radio on, and with the regular spot news some mention of the strike was always made. A fistfight had broken out on the wharf, but had been broken up with little harm done. More important, a conference had been arranged for that evening which, it was hoped, might bring matters to a head. If they were at the talking stage, there was some hope for an early settlement.

Though they were late getting home, Danny assured them his mother would have dinner waiting for them.

Danny telephoned the shipping office to see if any of the three were required for work, but was told they were not. He hung up, shrugging.

"I didn't think so. There are a lot of fellows without local connections who want to eat and sleep on the *Shamrock,* so there's plenty of help available."

When Mr. Beach came in, the visitors were introduced to him. He was attached to investigations, although he worked in uniform. He asked the boys how life was treating them, and Nelson reported one of his recent shipboard experiences.

"The first time I read a gauge, I reported the reading to the engineer, and he calmly went to the telephone and made a call to the bridge that we were about to blow up. The men went about shaking hands with each other and saying good-by, and wondering if they had their wills in order. They were all so cool and collected about it, I couldn't figure out what was happening. Finally, I caught on. I went back and got a correct reading, and believe me, my face was red while I did it."

But Ted was more interested just then in some of Mr. Beach's cases, and brought the conversation around to that subject when he could.

"Right now," said Mr. Beach, "I'm hunting for an escaped fire-bug by the name of Victor Wayne. I admit we often have trouble finding criminals when we don't know who they are, but when we do know it shouldn't be too difficult. We have his name, fingerprints, description, and usual method of operation. That should be enough."

"Suppose he went far away, changed his name and appearance, and took up a different line of work, then what would you do?" asked Nelson.

"You're supposing a lot of things that may not be possible for him," Mr. Beach explained. "He can change his name, of course, though this leaves him without any background, any references, which he may well need. He can make some changes in his appearance, but this may or may not be successful. Certain things remain pretty much the same—the outline of your face, the color of your eyes, your general build, but most of all your personality. Just imagine that Ted, here, did everything he could think of to change his appearance, and that you accidentally ran into him and talked with him. How many minutes would it be before a bell began to ring?

"You might say that he could go so far away he wouldn't be likely to run into anyone he knew, though you can't count on that in these days of rapid transportation. Even so, he's going to maintain some of his general interests, which may bring him into contact with people of the same interests, just as it did before. The police especially will be alerted, and may be following out some of these leads. Then there is money—he may not be able to afford to travel far, he may need work, and maybe the only work he is qualified for is the same thing he did previously. He may need to rely on old friends for help.

"And then, when you expect him to give up his criminal activities, you may be expecting far too much. Whatever misguided instincts led him into arson are likely to be still active within him. And if he is going to commit another crime, he is almost certain to commit one similar to the previous one. You see, criminals aren't particularly bright or versatile. If their last crime didn't work, they were probably caught; if it did work, they are likely to try it again.

"Finally, the fingerprints. He must be careful that he is never so much as suspected of another crime, or he will be fingerprinted and identified. That, too, may be way too much for him."

"I take it you expect to catch him," Nelson remarked.

"Oh, yes, I'm going to catch him, but I can't say how soon."

Later they turned on the news and this time it came up roses. The wildcatters had agreed to return to work the next morning, under the old terms, and their demands would be studied in connection with a new contract coming up at the end of the season.

"Yippee!" exclaimed Danny.

"Did you ever see anybody that happy to work?" Nelson demanded. "You'd think he hadn't been getting paid for loafing."

"But that wouldn't have gone on very long," Danny objected. "This way is safer."

"How soon do you think the *Shamrock* will be sailing?" asked Ted.

"They'll be bringing her down the river the first thing in the morning. Don't oversleep."

"No danger," said Nelson, half regretfully. "Ted's a regular alarm clock."

As Nelson had predicted, they had no trouble waking up early, and were down at the pier long before the *Shamrock* was towed out of the river. The tugs left her still inside the harbor, but directly facing the exit, so there would be no difficult turn for her to make. Danny arrived, and so did other sailors and some of their friends to see them off.

"Last boat going out," said the sailor in charge, as he looked around the group and checked off a list of names he was holding. When everyone was accounted for, he told them to get into the boat, and they shoved off into the harbor.

The lifeboat tied up at the fore end of the freighter, and they boarded her. Danny and Nelson hurried off aft to their quarters, and Ted reported to the deck crew for service. He was working outside when the vessel weighed anchor and steamed out into the open lake. It was an interesting, well-coordinated operation, with a lot of men rushing around, but each one knowing what he was supposed to do. Ted was assigned to help clean the decks from their traces of ore.

"Why are the hatch covers on if there's no cargo?" he asked Hansen, who was working next to him.

"Why not? You wouldn't want to fall into one of the holds, would you? Seriously, it's more shipshape that way, and of course you don't want any surplus water sloshing around in your holds."

Ted brought the captain's lunch, but the only thing he had to report was the rather doubtful information concerning the *Gray Lady.* Captain Weymouth said that he had known at least a dozen small boats of this name, though he had never heard of Captain Hunt. But whether he considered Ted's information significant or not, Ted had no way of knowing.

Taking his own lunch in the mess hall, Ted met Nelson, who informed him that Danny was now working the day shift, he had the swing shift, and a new man had been signed for the night shift.

"I haven't met him yet, but I suppose I will soon. Anyway I'm not the greenest hand down there now, so that'll be a big relief."

Naturally Nelson spent most of his free time taking pictures, and quite a number of the sailors asked to have their pictures taken so they might send copies home. Nelson was glad to oblige, and was soon making friends among the deck crew as well as among his own engine crew.

Fortunately Ted was still working on deck, and Nelson was not yet due on his shift, when the *Shamrock* turned north up the Detroit River, for this seemed too good a spectacle to miss. Nelson was active with his camera again, though with some regrets.

"I wish I was on shore and could get the *Shamrock* going by."

"Where on shore?" Ted returned. "You could only get two or three pictures and we'd be gone, and you'd be left behind."

Nelson agreed that he couldn't be everywhere at once, and would have to make the best of conditions as he found them. The vessel passed to the right of Bob-Lo Island and Grosse He, and to the left of strange, desolate Fighting Island, then turned northeast, past Zug Island at River Rouge, under majestic Ambassador Bridge and over the Detroit-Windsor tunnel—so they were told—and past Belle Island, Windmill Point, and Peach Island into Lake St. Clair.

"I notice we kept to the right, just the way we do on land," Nelson observed to one of the sailors.

"In the narrow passages we do, but out on the open lakes the shipping lanes have been laid out so that boats pass to the left. I don't know why that is, unless the down current is measurably stronger farther out in the lake."

As the freighter gave a fierce blast of its whistle, Nelson nodded approvingly.

"That's telling everybody to get out of the way. Nothing but a bigger boat would care to argue with that, and there isn't anything bigger on the lakes, is there?"

"Well, I do know of something else that can carry just as big a cargo as we can."

"You mean a freighter?"

"No, it isn't rightly a freighter."

"Some other kind of boat, then?"

"Hm, I don't think I'm going to tell you. You may have a chance to see for yourself on Lake Superior. If not, I'll tell you on the return trip."

They made several more guesses, including a pipe line, but he smilingly shook his head, and they were completely puzzled. Then he left.

"That steam whistle must be controlled from the bridge, even though it blows from the back," Nelson observed. "It reminds me of a rattlesnake listening for its own tail to rattle."

"Except that snakes are deaf," Ted came back.

"One thing you've got to say for these freighters—they seem to get the job done. Each end is independent but they work together."

Ted had supper with Danny, now off duty, who had some interesting news for him.

"I've just found out the name of the new wiper. Guess what it is."

"Grant?"

"Yes, Sam Grant. I haven't had a chance to talk to him yet, but maybe I'll find out how he got my number and what he wanted."

# CHAPTER 10.

## THE BOAT THAT WASN'T THERE

ARE you sure he's the one who called you?" asked Ted cautiously.

"Oh, I'm sure, all right, even though he didn't say so. But when we were introduced he gave me a wink, just as though we were old buddies. He's a few years older than I am, and a college graduate. I don't know why he's taking a job like this, since it doesn't look to me as though he intends to make a career of it."

"Maybe he's just friendly," Ted suggested. "Somebody gave him your name and number, and he thought he'd call you up to get acquainted."

"Maybe, but I don't know why that would call for a wink. Say, don't you think it's kind of spooky? Grant wouldn't be here if Star hadn't disappeared. Now Nelson and I—and this new Grant—are the wipers. How do we know something isn't going to happen to us?"

"You mean all the wipers disappear? You and Nelson look pretty solid to me—unless there's some reason why you want to disappear."

"Not me," said Danny with conviction. "I've got too much to look forward to. Well, it looks as though we won't have any trouble reaching Lake Huron before dark. I know the captain would rather negotiate the narrow passages between Erie and Huron during the daylight. There's less trouble with small boats, too."

"Aren't there more of them out in the daytime?"

"Yes, but the ones at night are more troublesome. A good many of them don't even carry proper lights."

Their day's work done, Danny and Ted stood at the rail to watch the passage into the St. Clair River, past Woodtick and Stag Islands, and finally under the Blue Water Bridge and out into broad Lake Huron. Out three miles ahead lay the lightship *Huron,* the only boat of its kind on the Lakes. They passed this, and there seemed nothing more to see that evening except empty water. As twilight closed in, the *Shamrock's* fights were turned on, a green fight to the right and a red light to the left. Amidships, the shadows were long, and reminded Ted of the scare he had had there once before. When Danny suggested turning in to their cabins, Ted was more than ready.

Mr. Bowling met Ted at the door to the companionway. "Going in?" he asked pleasantly.

"Yes, sir."

"I don't blame you. The evening's turning a little chilly. But before you do I have a little news for you. Better turn in early, because you'll be up at four. You will be serving a trick as quartermaster."

"Who, me?" Ted gulped. "I mean, yes, sir!"

Steering this big boat himself? He had never thought to see the day. And before dawn, too—the whole thing was scary. But he calmed down as he thought it over. Spanner Lines had millions of dollars invested in this boat, and they wouldn't be trusting it to an amateur. Undoubtedly there would be someone to supervise him closely.

"I won't be on the bridge myself. Ordinarily that would be my shift but the rotation has been moved up. Captain Weymouth always serves a trick on Lake Huron. It's not customary with captains, of course, unless one of the mates has a prolonged illness, and even then a papered man in the ranks is often promoted temporarily."

"Didn't the captain just serve on the bridge as we passed up the St. Clair River?"

"Oh, no. He was just supervising." Mr. Bowling laughed.

"But Captain Weymouth really takes charge when he takes over a shift on Lake Huron?"

"That's exactly what he does."

"Do you know any reason for it?" Ted wondered if he was being too free with an officer, but Mr. Bowling did not seem offended.

"The general opinion is that it brings back old memories to him. But I have my own theory." His voice lowered to a confidential level. "I don't think he likes the shipping lanes on Lake Huron. That's why he wanders off them."

"He does? Very far?"

The mate shrugged. "A matter of a few miles."

"Is that dangerous?"

"Obviously he doesn't think so. The down-bound shipping lane is seven miles east of the up-bound lane, so there is considerable leeway, unless we were to wander quite a few miles to the east at the same time that a down-bound vessel was wandering to the west. Then we might be in trouble—if we were blind; but we keep our eyes open."

"What about fog?"

"I'm sure Captain Weymouth wouldn't risk the vessel under conditions of poor visibility. He would stick to the regular lanes—though we still might get rammed from the back, or ram something ahead. There's nothing perfect."

He noticed Ted shivering, and said, "I'm keeping you out in the cold. You should be wearing your coat."

"It was warm when I came out. I guess I won't need my coat again tonight."

The mate held the door open for him as he went inside, then closed it after him. Ted's first impulse was to confide in Hansen, and he found him in their cabin. The old hand was reassuring.

"You're lucky to have a chance like that. Don't worry about anything. They'll tell you what to do. They try to give the new fellows a trick on the bridge as early as they can. It helps them get acquainted with what the boat's supposed to do, and how it's done. You never know when you may have to step up in an emergency."

"How closely does a boat have to stick to the regular shipping lanes?"

"Well, you want to avoid trouble, of course, but if you wander off a little out on the open lakes, either accidentally or for some purpose, it's no crime. It's just that if you do get into trouble, a somewhat greater share of the blame falls upon your shoulders. And of course the lights and maps and everything are intended to guide you along the regular lanes. It's different in the channels. Then you'd *better* be where you belong, if you know what's good for you."

"Then I'll be sticking exactly on the lane?"

"In all likelihood, unless you're ordered otherwise. There's some leeway for the officers. It's rumored that Captain Weymouth often deviates from course when he's on the bridge, but if he thinks he knows a better course that will save him a few hundred gallons of oil, what's there to argue about? I'm not sure the scheduled routes are always the best routes."

Ted was the first one to turn in in his cabin. For a time it was dark and deserted, as the off-duty crewmen gathered in one of the larger cabins where there was a television set. But presently the men drifted back, claiming that their story, which had come in so clearly as they passed a shore transmitter, had finally faded at the climax.

"I'll have to write to my wife and find out how it ended," one man grumbled.

Ted didn't mind their chatter, for he knew it was his excitement, more than anything else, which was keeping him awake. But finally he did drift off into a restless sleep. He woke up several times, and the third time found that it was ten minutes to four. He lowered himself quietly from his bunk, quickly dressed, and ran up to the bridge.

He found Captain Weymouth there, along with Lynn Kilbane, the part-time radio man who had apparently been acting as quartermaster. Ted learned he was to serve under the second mate, Mr. Keats, who arrived precisely on the hour. A few instructions passed between the captain and the mate, and Ted heard the master say:

"Let me know if we raise the *Washington.* I particularly want to speak her."

"Yes, Captain."

Kilbane turned the wheel over to Ted with a friendly grin, and for the first time Ted found his hands on the spokes. It felt firm to his touch, and he decided to simply hold it there until he was instructed otherwise. Then the captain and Kilbane left, and he was alone on the bridge with Mr. Keats. It seemed a heavy responsibility for just the two of them to be guiding this mammoth boat.

Of course Mr. Keats was aware of Ted's inexperience, and explained his duties to him with considerable patience and forbearance. He showed Ted how to read the compass, and how to hold to a course. Although there was an automatic pilot, or "iron mike," it was not being utilized at present. By the time these basic instructions had been given, Ted felt both more confident and considerably more at ease with Mr. Keats.

In between other duties, the mate showed Ted the rudder indicator, which showed the bridge at all times in what direction the rudder was pointing, the radio and direction finder, the radar, the telephone system, the whistle control, a Fathometer or echo-sounder for measuring depth, and alarms which were designed to give indications of trouble with leakage or fire anywhere on the boat. Ted also saw the companion to the clocklike dial they had already seen in the engine room.

He stared down at the water rushing past. "We seem to be going at a pretty good clip, sir. What's our speed?"

"We usually cruise at around seventeen miles per hour. Of course we're riding empty now, so we can make a little better time. The water ballast in the tanks makes up some of the difference. Our oil fuel is also a form of ballast, and we'll take on more water as the oil gets used up. Would you believe that we are using about one gallon of oil every six seconds?"

"What would happen if we didn't have ballast?"

"We just might flip right over, but don't let it worry you. It's never happened to us yet." He spoke as though this were good news. "Something like that did happen to the *Eastland,* I believe—an error in the ballast tanks and she overturned in the Chicago River. It was the greatest single disaster on the Lakes."

"I'm afraid I don't understand very well about who has the right-of-way, sir."

"That's a pretty tricky question, sometimes, for the rules get complicated. In the narrow channels the down-bound boat does, because it is under less rudder control than the up-bound boat." Ted nodded to show that he understood. "On the open lakes you have to know your seamanship—and have all the experience you can get. There are three basic situations: passing in opposite directions, overtaking, and crossing, and it depends on the angle of approach just which one applies. The boat approaching from the right has certain privileges, and sail has the privilege over motor because it is under poorer control. But you have to use common sense, too. Everybody knows these freighters can't stop on a nickel or turn on a dime."

Calls from the engine room, a radio message, and attention to his charts all took some of the mate's time—and he even left the bridge momentarily but soon returned.

"Turn her three degrees to the right," the mate ordered.

"Yes, sir," and Ted obliged—except that nothing happened! The *Shamrock* simply wasn't responding to the wheel. He turned it farther, and then gradually, in her own good time, the *Shamrock* began to turn. Then suddenly Ted realized, as the *Shamrock* overshot the mark, that he had turned too much, and he reversed the helm, but she kept going. Overanxious, he now turned back too far, and the *Shamrock* obliged by swinging back too much in spite of all he could do to stop her. It took a considerable amount of weaving back and forth before Ted had acquired the feel of the wheel.

Dawn on the lakes was an unforgettable experience. As the sky brightened, the Michigan shore became clearly distinguishable on the west, but to the east there was nothing showing except sky, water, and a few gulls. The air was crisp and seemingly clear. Then suddenly the sun, remembering its twilight promise to return, burst into the sky through colored streamers, and another day of endless possibilities had begun.

Lake Huron presented a vast emptiness, much like the ocean, Ted supposed. Still, it was considerably smaller than the ocean and the shipping lanes were more restricted. Wasn't it unusual that there would appear to be so little traffic out here, at the height of the shipping season?

Then he saw that they were not quite so alone as he supposed. On the horizon, on the down lane, another freighter was taking its plodding course through the water. A slight trace of morning haze still hung across the lake, and the boat was too far away to be distinguished clearly; but, as far as Ted could tell, it was a freighter very much like their own. It had the same distinguishing superstructures at the extreme ends, with the long flat deck between, and a single funnel from which he thought he could detect wisps of smoke.

He watched it for a while, then realized he had slipped a very small shade off his course, and set himself to rectifying his error without calling it to the attention of Mr. Keats. When Ted returned his attention to the freighter, he found it had disappeared. It was surprising that it should have passed out of his range of visibility in such a short time, but distances were deceptive, and the haze possibly thicker than it appeared.

He saw no reason to tell Mr. Keats of the passing freighter, which had been so far away from them as to offer no problem in navigation. Besides, although the second mate appeared to be busy drawing a line on a chart, Ted felt that very little escaped his attention.

With the coming of dawn activity increased. A light lunch was brought to them, and they ate as they worked. There were more telephone calls, and once Ted had to call Mr. Keats when there was the possibility of an encounter with a small boat. The mate stayed with him until the speedboat was past. Then, before he was aware of it, it was eight o'clock, and they were relieved.

Mr. Bowling came on the bridge, with a new helmsman whom Ted did not recognize.

"Did you spot the *Washington?*" Mr. Bowling asked. "The captain was particularly anxious about the water level in West Neebish Channel. He wants to know how big a load he can take on. The experts are predicting a seventy-five-million-ton season in ore, and we want to get our share of that."

"No, she hasn't passed down yet, sir," the second mate answered. "We haven't seen anything big all night."

About to speak, Ted caught himself in time. After all, it wasn't up to him to remind the second mate that they had passed another freighter within the last two hours. There might be more to this than met the eye, and if he didn't know what to say, it was better to keep his mouth shut.

# CHAPTER 11.

## THE RUMPUS IN THE ENGINE ROOM

TED was off duty that morning, and ate a late breakfast with Nelson. When Ted told of the freighter the second mate failed to report, Nelson was inclined to shrug it off.

"I can think of three simple explanations, Ted: he didn't see it, he forgot it, or he didn't think it was worth reporting."

"Well, I think he saw it, and I don't think he's in the habit of forgetting things like that; and if he didn't want to report it, all he had to say was that we hadn't passed the *Washington.* That would have been enough."

"What's your explanation?"

Ted shook his head. "That's the trouble, I don't have a good explanation. Why shouldn't he report it? If it wasn't the *Washington,* it wouldn't matter. And if it was the *Washington,* why didn't he say something? If the captain really needs that information, he's going to get it from somewhere, so this isn't going to hurt him any."

Nelson laughed. "You're trying too hard, Ted. Probably what happened is the second mate missed the *Washington* but didn't want to admit it. He wouldn't be the first person to try to cover up for himself. Why didn't you say something?"

"Because I didn't figure that was the best way to make friends and influence people and rise in the queen's navy. Common sailors don't contradict an officer."

On Ted's other problem, the captain's shift, Nelson could offer little help.

"I don't know whether that's very strange, a captain's serving a trick."

"But why always on Lake Huron?"

"Maybe it just turns out that way. It would have to be out on the open lakes somewhere, because he's usually on the bridge in the narrow channels anyway."

"And why does he change course?"

"Well, why not? He's the captain. If I had his stripes, I'd jolly well go where I wanted to. What's on your mind, Ted?"

"Just that maybe the two things go together. He serves a trick *because* it's important to change course. But why it should be important to change course for just a few miles I can't imagine."

"Whoa, Ted," Nelson cautioned. "We're not supposed to suspect the captain, remember? That's what Mrs. Dundee told us."

"I remember, and she ought to know him better than we do. But it could be that, without really doing anything wrong, he is still doing a favor for someone or being taken advantage of by someone."

"After all his years on the Lakes? You're crazy, Ted."

"Well, maybe, but whatever it is, I've got a hunch that Lynn Kilbane probably knows about it. It would be hard to hide it from him when they are both on the bridge together. And I'll bet you another thing—that Lynn Kilbane is always the quartermaster when the captain serves his trick."

Walking out along the stern, they encountered a sailor who seemed to have a few minutes to spare.

"Want to see what's pushing us?"

"Thanks, but we've seen the engine room already."

"No, I mean the propeller. Come on, take a look."

Obliged, they followed him around the deckhouse. Ted had previously noticed a canvas there, but had not thought to inquire what was beneath it. Now the sailor lifted one side. Held firmly into position by chains was a massive bronze casting of four blades, measuring some eighteen feet across. They were impressed.

"This is our spare," the sailor informed them. "What do you think of it?"

"I hope we never need it. How much does it weigh?"

"Three tons, give or take an ounce."

"I understand we only use one," Ted observed.

The sailor admitted it. "Why do you need more than one, when one will do the job? Seven thousand horsepower ought to be enough." He turned to Nelson. "Pardon me, but I couldn't help noticing your camera, and you looked as though you know how to use it. Would you be interested in taking some of me to send home?"

"Sure thing," and Nelson set to work. As he did, Ted made conversation.

"How are things going—smoothly?"

"Smoothly enough. Some of the men are grumbling because we're running shorthanded, but they're the kind who wouldn't be happy unless they were grumbling."

Ted realized that the men were paid by the length of the trip rather than by the hour; and therefore the fewer the men, the more work per man, at the same total pay.

"Are we really short of men?"

"It's not too bad, as long as we're running empty. That tugboat strike cost us some men who didn't want to wait around, but we'll probably be able to replace them at Duluth."

When the pictures were taken, the sailor gave his order, and wanted to pay for them in advance. It turned out that all he had was a twenty, but Ted offered to make change. He took out his wallet, looked in it, and suddenly changed his mind.

"I'm sorry, I don't seem to have it after all."

"Don't worry about it now," Nelson advised the sailor. "You'll be seeing me again."

"OK, then, and if you want a tip, Lake Superior is the best for fishing. There's a sea serpent somewhere up there. I never saw it myself, but I know some sailors that did. Perfectly sober, too."

The sailor returned to his duties with a cheery nod, but Nelson was anxious to get Ted aside.

"What happened, Ted?"

"My wallet's empty."

"How much did you have in it?"

"Just the twenty—a ten and two fives. I suppose I should be thankful he didn't take my driver's license."

Nelson was sympathetic. "Boy, that's bad. Where was your wallet?"

"In my coat. I left it hanging in the cabin a good part of the time. I suppose I should have taken my wallet with me."

"Well, Ted, I've got some money. I can help you out if you need it."

"No, there isn't much to spend money on aboard ship, and we'll be getting paid at the end of the trip. I just hate being stupid."

"And I hate losing money."

"Well, I don't suppose it's as bad as losing the Mississippi River," and Nelson was still chewing over this odd remark when their attention was drawn to the lake.

They were nearing the St. Marys River channel, and as the various shipping lanes converged, more and more boats came into view across the horizon.

The passage up the St. Marys River was an interesting experience. Passing the Detour Reef Light, they moved between Detour and Drummond Island, east of tiny Pipe Island and west of Lime Island, then followed the west coast of St. Joseph Island through an S-curve into Munuscong Bay, and up surprising Neebish Cut, where the water swelled up a hundred feet ahead of the boat. Past Neebish Island they entered narrow Lake Nicolet, passing west of Sugar Island, then swinging sharply westward to approach the Soo Locks. The river was now about three feet higher than at Lake Huron, the current two or three miles an hour, the shores wild and undesecrated. The river was half a mile wide below the locks, and here they paused long enough to get their instructions.

A signal told them to take the MacArthur Lock, next to the Michigan shore. While the *Shamrock* was passing through the lock, being raised twenty-one feet, Ted, Nelson, and other off-duty sailors were permitted to stretch their legs ashore. Nelson got some pictures of the carrier from the shore, against a dramatic backdrop, for the Soo Locks formed the busiest canal system in the world.

Back on board, they passed under the International Railway Bridge, then followed a long fifteen-mile curve to the head of the St. Marys River. Ted saw most of this, though he was obliged to report back to work after lunch. This time he was assigned to help clean holds.

The hatch cover was removed, revealing the big, empty cavern capable of holding more than a thousand tons of ore. The hold was washed out, dried, inspected for damage, and then the cover was replaced and they went on to the next one. It was tedious work, though it had to be done periodically.

After Nelson went on duty, Ted took supper up to the bridge as he usually did. Though he saw the captain, he made no formal report, nor did the captain seem to expect it. There would be time enough later, when Ted could gather all the fragments together, to submit a report.

Then Ted met Danny for supper.

"Boy, something went on in the engine room last night," Danny reported. "I hear Mr. Griffith almost took the roof off."

"I wouldn't have thought he ever raised his voice. What was it about?"

"It was Sam Grant. There's always a certain amount of tomfoolery going on, you know, but when it comes to the operation of the vessel, everyone is deadly serious. Anyway, Grant thought he had been ordered to clean out a certain valve, and started to take it out with a screw driver, but someone stopped him just in time. If he hadn't . . ."

"An explosion?"

"I don't know about that, but we'd have been stalled out here in the middle of nowhere for about a week while we waited for repair parts."

"What did Grant have to say about it?"

"He said he'd been ordered to do it by Mr. Griffith, and Mr. Griffith denied ever giving such a fool order as that. Since he's a licensed engineer, you have to go along with him. Boy, did he chew Grant out."

Ted considered. How did this fit into the long chain of mishaps which had been dogging the *Shamrock's* wake? Was it just a mistake, or was it sabotage? If it was sabotage, who was responsible, Grant or Mr. Griffith? He knew that Mr. Griffith enjoyed the captain's highest confidence—but then, if there was mischief afoot, it probably was being done by someone in whom everyone had confidence. It was hard to suspect Grant, who had joined the boat after many of these incidents had already happened. But Grant didn't seem to be exactly what he claimed to be, either, and that telephone call to Danny was still unexplained.

Ted was given the opportunity to look at the situation a little more closely when Grant came into the mess hall. Danny motioned to him to come over, and he did.

"Grant, this is a friend of mine from college, Ted Wilford—Sam Grant."

The two young men shook hands, though Ted sensed some reluctance on the part of the new wiper, for his handshake was limp, and he dropped his hand to his side a moment afterward. Danny did not seem to notice, but went on:

"You telephoned me at my home, didn't you, Grant?"

Grant's eyes were expressionless. "No, why should I do that?"

There was a moment of silent strain, which Ted sought to relieve with a light remark. "Maybe it was Lee, after all."

"My sister said somebody named Grant called," Danny went on. "I didn't know anyone of that name, until I was introduced to you yesterday."

Grant seemed rather standoffish. Apparently he felt he was intruding between Danny and Ted, and he soon made an excuse to take himself off. Loading up his tray, he took it outside.

"He seemed so friendly at first." Danny was plainly puzzled.

"All he did was wink," Ted reminded him. "That could mean almost anything."

"What I thought it meant was that we already knew each other, but I can see I was wrong about that. It seems that he doesn't know me any better than I know him."

Ted smiled. "My guess is that it's a case of mistaken identity. At first he thought he recognized you, then suddenly realized he was wrong. That's an odd coincidence about the name, though."

"Yes," Danny agreed, "and what I want to know is, if it wasn't this Grant who called me, who was it? Anyway, he could have been more friendly."

"If he's feeling the way I think he feels, right now he doesn't think he's got a friend in the world."

"Oh, come on, nobody's going to hold a simple mistake against him, especially when no harm was done. He'll realize that, after a while."

"But it may take time," Ted pointed out. "Anyway, I don't suppose they keelhaul offenders anymore or maroon them on a desert island."

"I haven't heard of it lately."

Then Ted recounted the story of his stolen twenty dollars, and asked, "Do you have much trouble with stealing?"

Danny shook his head. "Very little on a boat like this. There aren't too many people around—a lot fewer than on a passenger boat—and we're sort of a family. Besides, we don't have much around in the way of valuables. And then, if you were trying to steal something important, how would you get it off the boat? The chances are you'd be searched, and it would be found."

"A man doesn't have to allow himself to be searched if he doesn't want to."

"No, but if everybody else offers to be searched, where does that leave you?"

"Still, my money was taken."

"Did you mark it?"

"Yes, I had a *TW* up in the corner of each bill. But money can change hands, and a man can easily claim he acquired it innocently."

"But it doesn't change too fast on a boat, Ted, and you certainly wouldn't want it traced to you. Do you intend to report it?"

Ted had already considered that and decided against it. "I think I'd rather sit back and play a waiting game. But I can't help wondering if anything else has been stolen."

"Well, one of the men was bleating this morning about six candy bars being missing from his locker, but I wouldn't consider that stealing. It's more of a joke. You can't buy candy on board. Somebody will admit it later, and pay for them. I don't say it's right, but it's part of shipboard horseplay. In a family you share things like that, and I think it reminds some of the fellows of home."

They went out on deck and saw Grant eating by himself, but thought it better not to approach him just then. Instead, Ted remembered to ask Danny:

"A sailor was telling me there's something on the Lakes that can carry as big a load as one of these ore carriers. Do you know what it is?"

"Something besides a freighter? If he's not kidding, I can't imagine what it could be."

# CHAPTER 12.

## THE ALARM

THE problem of the two Grants was not to be solved immediately, but Ted soon uncovered another piece that only added to the puzzle. The passage across Whitefish Bay seemed uneventful, and he decided to return to his cabin for a while. If he could rest up for a time, he would be able to meet Nelson at midnight. Though he lay down on his bunk, his mind was active. The name Grant was still gnawing at him, and he felt sure he had run across it recently.

Finally it came to him. Spanner Lines issued small promotional booklets to employees and other interested persons. Hansen had one of these booklets, and had left it lying on the table in the cabin, where Ted had once picked it up and leafed through it. That must be where he had seen that elusive name. He slipped out of his bunk, and finding the booklet, went through it page by page. There it was, among a list of names over which his eye must have swept. William S. Grant was a member of the board of directors of Spanner Lines.

Well, where did this leave him? He now had three Grants to account for: the one who made the telephone call, the one serving in the engine room, and the one on the board of directors. Could all three be the same person? It was possible that William S. Grant had decided to use his middle name during his service on the *Shamrock,* but why should he work on a boat? On the other hand he seemed pretty young to be serving on the board of directors, though it might be possible if he had inherited a large block of stock. A more likely explanation was that Sam Grant was the son of William S. Grant, and had gone to work on one of the company boats for some special reason. What was it? Simply to get experience, or was he there on behalf of a minority group of stockholders who were dissatisfied with Mrs. Dundee's management?

Hansen came in, but made no comment on Ted's use of the booklet. He waited till Ted had replaced it, then remarked:

"How did your trick on the bridge go?"

"Pretty well, I guess."

"Right on course?"

"As far as I know."

"Then you do better than the captain. I heard another story about that today."

As long as this particular trait of the captain was already well known to ship scuttlebutt, there seemed to be no reason why Ted shouldn't comment on it.

"Do you know why he does it?"

"I only know why they say he does it. He's searching for sunken treasure." Hansen said this with a perfectly straight face, and Ted was uncertain whether to accept it without salt, or put it in the same category as the Lake Superior sea serpent.

"How would that help him find treasure?"

"He keeps the Fathometer going constantly. That gives him readings of the depths. Well, if he takes enough readings, he may find them jumping unexpectedly for a short space. That means he's located some big bump on the bottom of the lake—maybe a sunken boat."

"Then what would he do?"

"If he were in a smaller boat he would sail back and forth over it until he had figured out its dimensions, and from that he might be able to deduce what boat it was. If it's the one he's looking for, he's in business. Of course he can't do that on a big freighter that doesn't belong to him, but he can mark down the location and come back to it later."

"This sounds like the old days of the Spanish galleons," said Ted with a smile, "except that I don't suppose these lake boats ever carried gold."

Hansen looked mysterious. "Don't count on it. Now that ocean ships are coming into the Lakes, they might be carrying bullion. And even so there's the boat's safe, which might contain jewels or coins. Paper money would be in a bad way, I suppose, unless it was awfully well protected, but nobody ever expects a boat to sink."

"Would there be some chance of salvaging the boat or its cargo?"

"There might be, especially if it wasn't in too-deep water. Even then they might be able to get a hose down to her and pump oil out of her tanks."

"And iron ore?"

"I guess not," said Hansen regretfully. "It would be too expensive to salvage from deep water. When you think of the value per ton—"

This remark was never finished, for a shrill alarm rang out, causing them to jump.

"What is that?" asked Ted.

"If it's like other fire alarms I've heard, that's what it is. Come on, let's git. Got anything valuable?"

Ted had nothing worth worrying about except his coat, which he snatched up. They ran out on deck. Many sailors were scurrying about, but there was no sign of smoke. The alarm had apparently sounded from the bridge, but whether the fire had been pinpointed or not, they could not tell.

They overheard one of the sailors saying, "It's back near the engine room somewhere. The automatic sprinklers went on."

Ted turned to Hansen for guidance.

"Let's go to our lifeboat stations," he advised. "They'll know where to find us if they want more men. Meanwhile, there's no use cluttering up things."

The freighter was out of sight of land, and Ted supposed they had probably passed beyond Whitefish Bay and out into Lake Superior. His mind raced through all the contingencies. Suppose the fire spread, could all the personnel be saved? They could if all the lifeboats could be lowered into the water, but what if some of them were damaged? He was glad to see, however, that though there seemed to be a good deal of activity and confusion, no one appeared panicky. There was still no sign of smoke, and no attempt was being made to launch the lifeboats, even at the stern, so the chances were things would soon be under control.

A sailor called down from the bridge, "You can relax, everybody, the fire's out."

Apparently his news came over the telephone from the engine room, and seemingly it was accurate. Everybody seemed to be walking slower, as though there was no great rush about anything.

"What was it?" someone asked the sailor on the flying bridge.

"Just a fire in a wastebasket down in the carpenter's room. Some-one must have tossed a match or a cigarette into it. It was a metal container, and there wasn't much danger of its spreading, but the heat was enough to touch off the sprinklers. Those fellows back there are going to have a mopping-up job to do."

After the short excitement of the fire, the rest of the evening seemed an anticlimax. When Danny came forward, he explained a little about the fire.

"Nothing much to see, Ted, but nobody had any business being in the carpenter's room at that time. It wasn't the carpenter or his helper."

His account of the fire substantiated what Ted had already learned, except that Danny was less certain the fire was harmless.

"I know it was a metal wastebasket, but there were shavings around, and the heat through the metal might have started them on fire."

"How do you figure it—deliberate or accident?"

"Oh, probably an accident, but darned careless of somebody. One of the fellows on duty may have ducked in there for a quick smoke, and then had to get out fast. I don't see how it could be deliberate, because it might not have caught on the shavings, especially with the automatic sprinklers ready to go into action. Somebody wanting to start a fire would have done a better job of it than that."

"Unless he was interrupted before he could do it thoroughly," Ted pointed out.

"I suppose there's that," and Danny grew very thoughtful.

A sailor, whom Ted knew only by the nickname of Boze, came up to them and said to Danny, "Aren't you the one who asked to see my stamp collection sometime?"

"Why, yes, I am," Danny returned, in some surprise as though he had forgotten making such a request.

"I've got it on board with me now, and I'm not doing anything. Want to come down—you and your friend?"

They agreed and accompanied Boze down to the forecastle. The sailor got out his album and explained some of the special finds in his collection, then said:

"Wait till I get my reading glass and you'll be able to see some of the finer details on these."

But he couldn't find it.

"Come on, fellows," he said to the men around him, "I know somebody lifted my reading glass. Now where is it?" No one answered, and his voice became stronger. "If you give it back now I won't say a word, but if you don't . . ."

The threat failed to produce the hoped-for result, but another sailor drawled, "Maybe it's the same place as my red bandanna."

They returned to a study of the stamps. In many instances there were two which seemed identical, though one was valuable and the other nearly worthless.

"I could show you the differences if I had my lens," Boze complained.

Because of his annoyance, they enjoyed themselves less than they had expected and left sooner than they would have otherwise.

"Another theft," Ted pointed out. "Have you heard anything more, Danny?"

"Not actually. I did hear the steward complain about somebody messing around with his stores, but simmer down. That's nothing strange on shipboard. Somebody's always looking for a snack at odd hours."

"Would the door to the storeroom be locked?"

"Probably not. They don't go much for locked doors on shipboard. You never know when some kind of emergency may come up and you'll want to get in fast. You won't have time to fool around hunting for keys."

The engine room had been stuffy all day, and Danny was agreeable to a turn on deck before turning in.

"Cool, isn't it? Would you believe that sometimes there are icebergs on Lake Superior?"

"You have to be kidding," Ted retorted.

"Well, not the classic kind of icebergs, maybe. But the wind piles up the ice at Whitefish Bay, and sometimes it breaks off and floats around. That's after the shipping season is closed, so it's no particular menace. You know, Lake Superior never freezes over, though Erie sometimes does. After the first icing-up, the Coast Guard spends most of its time chasing children off the ice. They don't realize how dangerous it might be."

Having grabbed some sleep, or the next thing to it, Ted was up to meet Nelson as he planned. It was the fire, of course, which was most strongly on his friend's mind.

"About all I could think of was that I was glad this wasn't an oil tanker."

"We've got plenty of oil on board—in the fuel tanks."

"That's right. Wasn't I lucky I didn't think of that?"

But Nelson had a more personal gripe on, and after he had picked up a snack in the mess hall, he told Ted about it.

"Ted, my case of camera filters has been stolen!"

"Filters? What would anyone do with those?"

"They might use them on their cameras, you know."

"But I thought they were a special size."

"Well, they wouldn't fit all cameras, of course, and some people with cameras who aren't exactly shutterbugs wouldn't even want to bother with them. But someone might have a use for them. There are quite a few cameras on board. I noticed especially that Sam Grant has a camera similar to mine, though he doesn't seem to use it very much."

"Grant!" Ted exclaimed.

"Now wait a minute, Ted, I'm certainly not going to accuse him just because he owns a camera. But how many things have been stolen so far?"

Ted enumerated them. "My twenty dollars, some candy bars, perhaps some ship's stores, a red bandanna, a magnifying lens, and your camera filters. That may not be everything, of course. Maybe some of the sailors haven't bothered reporting small losses, and maybe there are some big losses that have been quietly reported to the officers and nothing has been said about them."

Nelson pondered for a moment. "There's a lot of stuff there that doesn't amount to a hill of beans, Ted. Maybe there's a kleptomaniac on board. You know how those people help themselves to anything that takes their fancy, and very often it's something of practically no value."

"Most of the men have sailed with the *Shamrock* before, and according to Danny there's never been any trouble over stealing. These thefts only seem to have started within the last few days."

Having decided to take a little walk on deck before retiring, Nelson stopped in his cabin for a sweater. As they were passing the storeroom toward the stairs they thought they heard a slight scuffling inside. They stopped in their tracks. The door was closed, and there was no light on inside.

"Do we or don't we?" asked Nelson in a whisper.

"We do!"

"Then go!"

They flung the door wide open and stood in the doorway, staring in. Caught by the beam of the light from the passageway, Sam Grant spun about, looking startled.

"I thought I heard a noise in here," he explained. "I came in to investigate."

"Without a light?" asked Ted.

"Oh, I had the light on a moment ago. Then I turned it off and pretended to leave, just to see if anything would happen."

"Aren't you supposed to be on duty?" Nelson reminded him.

"I sure am. But I was sent on an errand that took me by here. Well, I'd better be heading back before you-know-who blows another gasket. So long."

He left the room as they stepped aside for him, and hurried back in the direction of the engine room. Ted and Nelson looked at each other, and then with one accord turned the light on and closed the door behind them.

Their search was thorough, they thought, but completely unproductive. There just didn't seem to be any place in the room where anyone could be hiding. There were a great many cartons of food, still sealed up, and more that were open, but all these were still well filled. They tested every box large enough to hold a person to make sure no one was hiding there. They looked behind each box for a possible place of concealment. There was no one besides themselves in the room, they were convinced. They switched off the light and stepped outside, closing the door after them.

"We don't want to get caught here ourselves," Ted observed, "and get in the steward's doghouse."

"I wonder if Grant really did hear anything in there?" Nelson speculated.

"He said he did. Why else would he have gone in?"

"I know what he said, but all we found was Grant. But I can't think what he might have been up to. He couldn't be hungry. We get plenty to eat."

They walked upstairs and out onto the deck, giving a nod to the watch. They were not alone, for many of the men just getting off work had taken a little snack up on deck, and were eating, exercising, and getting some fresh air before turning in.

At an isolated spot on the deck, they stood by the railing, breathing deeply.

"You know," Neslon began, musingly, "it's possible Grant was telling the truth. I don't know why else he would have gone in there. And if he is, then he really did hear something."

"Only we didn't find anything," Ted pointed out.

"I know, but it's easy enough to make a mistake about *where* the noise was coming from."

"In that case he might have been mistaken about what sort of noise it was, too. It could have been the engine or one of the pipes or something like that."

"Yes, but he seemed to think it was a person and that it was worth investigating. All right, let's suppose he knows what he's talking about. That means there's a pretty good chance for a stowaway on board."

Ted gave Nelson's idea some careful study, but had some objections to make. "Why a stowaway, necessarily? It could have been a member of the crew."

"Well, let's look over that list of things that were taken again. A stowaway knows he's going to need money sometime, so that accounts for your twenty dollars. I'm pretty sure you're not the wealthiest person on board, but maybe you were the handiest, and he helped himself. Now the candy bars and food from the storeroom. No one except a stowaway would have to be so worried about getting something to eat. You might ask why he doesn't steal from the mess hall, but there are fellows coming and going there at all hours. He might not be able to take a chance."

"What about the other things that were stolen?" Ted inquired.

"Well, he might just have helped himself to whatever came to hand. In the dark, he might not even have been sure what it was.

He might have thought my camera filters in their leather case were something valuable that he could sell later."

"What about your theory that there is a kleptomaniac on board?"

"Couldn't the stowaway be a kleptomaniac, too? There are only two reasons I can think of why a person should stow away: because he's hiding out or because he wants to get somewhere. If he wanted to get somewhere why should he stow away on an ore carrier?"

"Suppose he wanted to get to Duluth—or maybe just anywhere that was far enough away?"

"All right, how does he do it? His chances of getting ashore at Duluth are pretty slender, from what I hear. We're only there for a couple of hours, I understand, and everybody's around topside and busy as beavers. And it's all in daylight, too. You might say the same thing for the St. Marys River and the Detroit River—they like to work in daylight as much as they can. So he gets on board, finds that there's no chance to get ashore except in broad daylight, and there he is back home again. It has to be that he's in hiding." He paused to let Ted consider his ideas. "How does that sound to you?"

"It may be just as good as any theory I've been able to dream up. I've been sort of looking at it in a different way. A reading lens was stolen and there was a fire. Probably the glass was stolen first, even though it wasn't missed till afterward. Does that suggest anything to you?"

"You mean somebody started the fire with sunlight through a lens? I can't imagine a man doing anything like that. That's a typical kid's stunt."

"Maybe, but that doesn't necessarily rule out an adult. But going over the list of stolen things again, a red bandanna and your filters are the kind of things that might appeal to somebody young. If the things were stolen by an adult, it could have been anyone; you don't have to imagine a stowaway then. Actually, it's that neat relation between the stolen lens and the fire that makes me believe there could be a stowaway aboard."

"How do you figure the fire, then, Ted?"

"I can't see it as a serious effort to set the boat on fire, unless, of course, the person was interrupted. It could have been an accident— somebody just playing around. Or it could have been a diversion.

Somebody wanted to create attention here to take attention away from somewhere else."

"When that fire alarm went off, Ted, everybody's attention was everywhere. And if you wanted a diversion, why not use a match? You don't need a reading lens."

Ted laughed. "Well, there are certainly plenty of objections, no matter which way you turn. I can't see much point in these thefts, for a stowaway or anyone else."

"If there is a stowaway, Ted, I don't think it could be a boy. A boy running away from home and stowing away on a boat would have to worry about keeping hidden, providing for himself, and the consequences after he was found. He wouldn't have much time to fool around starting a fire with a lens."

"Not all kids worry about consequences. A boy doesn't always run away from home because he's unhappy. He might simply be out for a lark."

"Another thing that would make it difficult for a boy is that he wouldn't dare be seen at all, not even at a distance. If there is a boy on board, he'd probably need the help of some adult, and I can't quite picture that, either. But whoever it is, I'm sure there's somebody on board who doesn't belong here."

# CHAPTER 13.

## THE GRAY LADY AGAIN

BUT supposing there was a stowaway on board, what could they do about it?

"We can't launch another general search on the basis of the little information we've got now. And when you think of where he might be hiding, there are probably hundreds of places he could squirm into, though he'd certainly have to come out sometime."

"How about one of the lifeboats, Ted?"

"It could be. Daytime would be the best time to check. He'd have to hole up when it was light."

"Then if he's wandering around the boat, Ted, night would be the best time to come across him. Let's keep our eyes open."

With this in mind they wandered up and down the decks several times through the overcast, chilly night. But Ted at last decided he needed sleep if he was going to be any good for the next day's work. Nelson thought he would try a little longer, though things did not look promising; the deck was too long and had too many shadows.

"If we're going to find him, Ted"—Nelson no longer spoke as though he had any doubts about the stowaway—"we're going to need some luck."

Ted fell asleep promptly, and for a few hours slept the sleep of the just. But he was not destined to slumber uninterrupted during the remainder of the night. Some slight rustling near his bunk aroused him, and he awoke with a start, holding his breath. He could hear heavy breathing from the other bunks, so it was likely he was the only one awake.

There was definitely someone in the cabin. He was feeling his way about, guided by his sense of touch and the slight moonlight shining through the porthole. Whatever the intruder wanted, he did not seem to be working haphazardly. He passed the table and some of the lockers where he might have been able to pick up a little loot. Instead he made his way almost directly to the spot where Ted's coat was hanging.

Ted thought of crying out, but decided against it. He felt sure the thief would escape before anyone was awake enough to pursue him. Besides, anyone going into Ted's wallet was due for a bad letdown: someone had been there before. Ted decided it was more important to try to identify the man than to interfere with him.

The thief put his hand smoothly into Ted's coat pocket and extracted his wallet. He went through it quickly, holding it up to the light of the porthole, and as he did so Ted caught a glimpse of his face. Then the wallet was replaced in the pocket, and the man glided out of the room.

For nearly an hour Ted lay there thinking, almost in a state of shock. Though not positive, he was pretty certain that the thief was Lynn Kilbane! But what was he after, what did he want? Was it money, and had he been surprised to find there was none, and then left? It was hard to see what else he could have been after, for the wallet contained nothing except Ted's driver's license and perhaps a couple of other small things, but the thief had had no opportunity even of reading them in that dim light.

Ted fell asleep at last, and was awakened again by the bustle about the cabin as another working day started. He remembered the nocturnal visitation, and decided he'd better check his wallet the first thing. Then he remembered: his press card! Was that what Kilbane had wanted to see? Ted was not on board the *Shamrock* officially as a reporter, but did Kilbane suspect it, or at any rate suspect something and want to find out who Ted really was? The only trouble was that Ted was sure Kilbane hadn't been able to read anything in the near-dark. If this was his objective, he would have taken it with him, but all the papers were intact.

Then, idly, Ted checked the money compartment. It was no longer empty! It now contained a ten-dollar bill and two fives. Just to make sure, Ted checked for his initials in the corners, and found them there. These were the very same bills which had been stolen.

This was certainly a most curious thief. Had he repented, and was now trying to make good on his misdeeds? But Nelson's filters had been stolen, apparently that same night while he was on duty. What sort of thief was this who returned one thing while taking another?

Ted brought the officers' breakfast, and had no fresh news from the captain except that he had checked by radio and learned that John Star's body had not yet been found. Then Ted went for his own breakfast—late, thereby missing Danny, who had to report for work at eight, and Nelson, who was sleeping late. Ted was not worried, knowing that Nelson was usually a late sleeper when he could be, and not much of a breakfast eater anyway. But he did wonder just how long he had stayed on patrol.

That was the morning that stories began to spread throughout the length of the *Shamrock* that the vessel was haunted. Ted heard the story from several people, but could not tell how the thing had started. The ghost had been seen here, it had been seen there. It was the ghost of a sailor who had been washed overboard years ago, it was the ghost of a tyrannical captain who had been fired, it was . . . but each story was different. All Ted knew was that he had never heard mention of a ghost before, and now suddenly everyone was talking about it. Surely something must have happened to touch things off—possibly, Ted thought, some sign of the stowaway.

During the course of the morning he checked the lifeboats both fore and aft and found them undisturbed. The canvas covers were still tied with neat sailors' knots, so there could be no one inside, unless someone else had taken the trouble to fasten him in. He dared probe no further.

A curious phenomenon appeared that morning, far out over the clear blue water.

"What's that, whales?" asked Ted, incredulous, of Hansen.

"No, but something almost as remarkable. Those are waterspouts."

"What makes them?"

"The worst kind of waterspout is made by a tornado touching down into the water or coming mighty close. I don't think most waterspouts are that bad. You've seen summer whirlwinds that pick up a paper and toss it around. If they get strong and steady enough, they could pick up a column of water, just the way they pick up sand over a desert. Of course you can call any whirling wind a tornado if you want to."

"Are waterspouts dangerous?"

"The milder ones are considered harmless. They could upset a small boat, but usually you'd have no trouble maneuvering out of their way."

The spouts had attracted the interest of other sailors on deck, who were calling out to their mates to come and see them. The columns, far enough off so that they appeared to offer no possible threat to the *Shamrock,* seemed to frolic playfully for a time, then suddenly collapsed and disappeared.

"You're playing in luck this trip," Hansen observed. "You don't see waterspouts every day on the Lakes, or even every season."

"Have you ever seen them before?" Ted questioned.

"Just once—years ago, from the shore of Lake Erie."

They had passed the Apostle Islands and were making their approach to the lakehead at Duluth-Superior. The highlands of Duluth were an enticing sight, and doubtless offered a magnificent view of the cresent-shaped harbor, nearly landlocked with a long sand bar, through which there appeared to be two cuts, one of them crossed by the famed Aerial Bridge. Across St. Louis Bay lay the flat ground of Superior, Wisconsin.

Neither Danny nor Ted would be able to go ashore; the one was on duty in the engine room, the other busy on deck. Nelson, however, was free. He decided against a quick souvenir trip of Duluth—although a number of sailors set out with that in mind—and chose to hang around taking pictures instead. He had time for a few words with Ted, and said that he had been on patrol till about 3 A.M., until the watch seemed to be growing suspicious of him and he thought it better to retire.

Ted was busy as a beaver, helping with the hatch covers under the direction of the deck boss, but still found time to admire that immense machinery which poured ore into the holds as though it were sand and the boat a child's toy. The ore even conveyed a distinctive odor which he was beginning to recognize.

No time was wasted in port. The hatch covers were still being fitted back into place as they cleared harbor.

The answer to the sailor's riddle came that afternoon, and it was Hansen himself who called it to Ted's attention. Far out across the lake, toward the Canadian side, a strange object rode in the water.

It was too far away to be seen clearly, but Hansen brought a pair of binoculars to their assistance. Even after he had looked through the glasses, Ted was uncertain what it was.

"Two tugboats seem to be pulling and pushing at something or other. What is it?"

"What does it look like?" asked Hansen.

"If I didn't know better, I'd say it looked like a floating island."

"And you wouldn't be far wrong about that, Ted. Actually, it's a floating island of lumber. There's a big island of logs, and around the perimeter there is a sort of fence, or loop, of logs tied together to hold the whole thing in one mass."

"And there's as much lumber in that island as there is ore on this freighter?"

"By weight, probably yes, and by bulk it is even larger. This freighter couldn't hold all the wood in that island."

"Yes, I can sort of distinguish individual logs, now that I know what they are. That is something," and Ted handed back the binoculars to him for another look.

"You were lucky to see it," Hansen remarked. "Naturally, they don't want a thing like that clogging up the shipping lanes, so they keep their distance."

"Any chance the island might break apart?" asked Ted.

"I sincerely hope not. They'd have a real mess on their hands."

"This is as interesting as a sea serpent," Ted decided. "I suppose you can't help me there?"

"It depends on whether you want a story or pictures," said Hansen good-naturedly, and took his departure.

By late afternoon Ted had reached a decision. He was going to have it out with Kilbane. That the radio man had stolen his money and then replaced it made no sense, and the simpliest way to find out why was to ask him.

He encountered Kilbane on his way to the mess hall.

"Thanks, Kilbane."

The radio man stopped and looked at him skeptically. "Thanks for what?"

"For returning my twenty dollars to me. Where did you get it?"

Kilbane made no effort to lie his way out.

"You saw me, then?"

"I don't suppose you stole my money just for the purpose of giving it back, so that means you didn't steal it."

"That's right." Kilbane hesitated. "But if I told you where I got it you wouldn't believe me anyway."

"Try me and see."

Kilbane decided to risk it. "Well, then, I found it in my wallet!" Ted showed his surprise. "Yes, in my wallet," he repeated. "I had twenty dollars of my own—and some more besides, but something about this money made me look at it more closely. Then I saw that it didn't have my marks on the bills, but they did have someone else's. What was I supposed to think? Somebody had gone into my wallet, but he hadn't stolen my money. Oh, no, he had just substituted somebody else's. That could mean only one thing. I was going to be accused of stealing somebody else's money. Somehow an excuse would be made to look into my wallet, and it would be discovered that I was holding money that had been previously stolen from someone else. Then the soup would be in the fire. What was I to do? You know that a lot of people think I faked that radio message that sent us on to Buffalo, and I certainly couldn't afford another black mark on my record. The captain's been showing confidence in me, and I didn't want to shake it. He promised to help me get my mate's papers. I decided that the only thing to do was to return the money."

"How did you know to whom to return it?"

"I found the initials *TW* in the corner. I inquired around, and you were the only person on board with those initials."

Ted considered. As far as he could tell, every note of Kilbane's story rang true.

'Tell you what, you're out twenty dollars now, and you didn't have to be. What do you say we split the difference, ten apiece?"

Kilbane didn't want to do it, but at last consented to accept the bill.

"Maybe I'd better tell you something else that happened to me. Going through my study papers, I found a little booklet that didn't belong to me. It was one of those folders from Beatrice Lines. I'm sure somebody planted that on me, so it would look as though I was acting as a spy for the other company. Everybody knows that if we lose this contract, Beatrice Lines will probably pick it up."

"What did you do with the booklet?"

"Don't worry, I got rid of it overboard, the first chance I got. Nobody was going to find that thing on me. As long as I'm working for Spanner Lines, I'm loyal to Spanner Lines."

They went off to the mess hall together, but separated there to eat with their own friends.

Ted saw no harm in telling Danny of the return of his money. He went on to explain the theory—his and Nelson's—that there was a stowaway on board.

Danny listened patiently. "It seems to me that you both believe in the stowaway, but for different reasons."

"Well, what do you think?"

But Danny refused to commit himself to the idea, nor was he buying the ghost stories which had suddenly sprung to life. But he did agree to make some effort to patrol the deck, in the hours before midnight.

"After that it's up to you and Nelson. You can do whatever you like."

Ted slept as well as he could during the evening, then got up at midnight to meet Nelson as usual. They ate, walked, and talked on the dark deck. Though no sign of a stowaway appeared, as they stood at the stern for several minutes, Nelson exclaimed:

"Want to know something, Ted? There's a motorboat out there shadowing us."

"You sure? I don't see anything."

"No, but she's there. She must have come a little closer than she planned, realized she was visible from our deck, and fallen back again."

"The *Gray Lady?*"

Nelson shrugged. "Your guess is as good as mine. If it was the *Gray Lady* you saw in the harbor, this could be the same boat."

"If it is, she must have followed us all the way up the Lakes."

"But why, Ted?"

"That's a good question, and I can think of two answers. One, she's waiting her opportunity for something. Two, she's checking up on us to see what we're about."

"Well, what are we about? Everybody knows where we're going and what we're doing. There's no secret about that."

"No?" Ted raised his eyebrows. "What about the *Shamrock's* occasionally deviating from course, while Captain Weymouth is in charge of the bridge? Somebody may want to know more about that."

"Would they know when Captain Weymouth is taking a trick?"

"They might, if somebody on the *Shamrock* tipped them off."

"If they know that much, then they ought to know it only happens on Lake Huron. Then why are they still following us here?"

"I gave you two suggestions. Try the other one."

But just what sort of opportunity the *Gray Lady*—if it were she—was waiting for they could not guess. The other time she had come up quite close to the *Shamrock* then sped away, apparently without accomplishing anything. Was it her intention to approach closely again, and complete the mission that had been interrupted before? If so, her opportunities were less favorable, for a better watch was maintained while the boat was in motion than while it was anchored in harbor.

"What's way out there before you reach Canada?" asked Nelson.

"Thunder Bay, I guess, if you go far enough."

"I thought we passed Thunder Bay on Lake Huron."

"That was a different one. I think there's one on Lake Erie, too."

It was a spooky feeling to know that there was a boat out there, without knowing just what it was up to. If Ted was inclined to doubt Nelson's vision, he did not doubt it a little later when they had made another turn around the deck and this time, standing at the stern, he himself saw a boat of some kind, apparently still following them and still maintaining its distance. A sudden break in the clouds letting the moon shine through was responsible; otherwise he might not have seen it. As it was, the motorboat immediately dropped back again.

"She must be breaking the navigation laws," Nelson decided, "running without lights. Are we in Canadian or American waters?"

"I don't know, but I imagine it's against the law to run without lights, no matter which country you're in."

"That means she can't take a chance on being seen."

"But we did see her, Nel," Ted pointed out, "twice. It may mean that she would prefer not to be seen, but if she is it can't be helped. She's going to stick on our tail no matter what."

They checked again later, but this time the motorboat had either given up the chase or was staying discreetly out of sight.

"I can't figure this out at all, can you, Ted?"

"I can think of a possible explanation," said Ted thoughtfully, "but that doesn't mean it's the right one. Maybe somebody is supposed to drop a bundle overboard, and the *Gray Lady* is supposed to pick it up."

"Would they be able to find it in the dark?"

"Maybe they could if it had some sort of signal—maybe an ultraviolet light or a radio signal, or something of that kind."

"Do you think it's happened already?"

"I wouldn't know, but if it hasn't it may be because we interfered. We've been out on the decks pretty steadily now, and the person supposed to drop the bundle may not have had a good opportunity. But this is all speculation. The real answer might be completely different."

As the motorboat remained out of sight for some time, they took another complete turn around the deck, to see whether it might be attempting to approach them from another side.

"There it is again," Nelson insisted, "still out there. I can hear the engine."

"I can hear something," Ted agreed, "but it could be just an echo of our own engine. Listen again. What do you think?"

"I'll tell you what I think—somebody's due for a surprise. They've spotted her up on the bridge, and they're bringing the searchlight around. They'll be snapping it on in a moment."

With this warning, the glaring light did not startle them, but it appeared to startle the occupant of the shadowing boat. Now caught in the full glare of the beam, all its attempts at secrecy were lost. The pilot gunned his motor and swung about, and this time the name on the back panel definitely read *Gray Lady*.

The strange boat had been driven off and disappeared into the black night. Pursuit would have been impossible, since the *Gray Lady* was both faster and more maneuverable; anyway, the carrier could not be diverted from its principal mission, which was to get its load of ore down to the hungry steel mills just as soon as possible.

"Well, is there a stowaway or isn't there?" Nelson demanded, as they decided to abandon their watch.

"I don't know," Ted answered with a tired smile. "Let's sleep on it, and see how things look in the morning. One thing I think is sure: we've seen the last of the *Gray Lady*. Now that she's been identified at least by name, her pilot would never dare bring her in close to the *Shamrock* again. He's probably scooting for home."

"Wherever home is, Ted."

# CHAPTER 14.

## A CHASE

NEXT day Ted was given a painting assignment that kept him outside and also relieved him of the duty of serving the meals to the officers. He was busy at work on the deckhouse, standing on a low scaffold, when he saw something out ahead.

"Is that a boat?" he asked of the sailor next to him.

"No, it's the Groscap Light, where the St. Marys River begins. It's a common mistake. You must have missed it coming up."

This answer came unexpectedly from Mr. Bowling, who had paused for a moment beneath the scaffold.

"The captain wants you to go ashore with him at the Soo," Mr. Bowling went on, "so you'd better get that paint scraped off of you in plenty of time."

Ted thanked him and, when the time came, was glad to leave the rest of the painting job to his colleagues. He had thought they might question his assignment with the captain, but found out it was exactly what they expected. The captain's messboy was expected to act as "legs" for him whenever there were any errands to run. Ted had wondered before why one of the mess hands did not bring the officers' meals forward; but mealtime was their busiest time, and it was better done by someone else who could be assigned to other duties between meals.

He left the boat with the captain, and was informed that they were to stop in at the Coast Guard station. There was a decision for the captain to make: whether he should order the *Shamrock* to wait until he returned, or send it on ahead without him. This was the height of the shipping season, and he had confidence in Mr. Bowling, so he ordered that they should proceed as fast as they could. If he was left behind, he would be able to overtake the carrier in a motorboat.

There was a delay waiting for Lieutenant Commander Lehigh of the Coast Guard—and Ted thought it was a relief, finally, to meet someone in charge who wasn't a captain. It meant, though, that the *Shamrock* would be leaving without them. During the interval Captain Weymouth explained to Ted what they were doing.

"I've been taking depth readings on Lake Huron, a little off the established trails. The Coast Guard, of course, wants as complete a record of the lake as it can get, so every additional set of readings helps. They can't do it all themselves; in fact, their major efforts are directed toward the shallow channels."

"I understand, Captain." Ted understood a lot of things. The captain's wanderings from the regular lanes could hardly be questioned if he was on a Coast Guard assignment. "Was there anything secret about this mission?"

"About the mission itself, no, Ted, but the results, yes. Comprehensive readings of this kind may turn up the location of long-sunk wrecks, and some of these wrecks could have a value to the insurance companies. Rather than pave the way for adventurers and reward-seekers, the Coast Guard prefers that each wreck be identified if possible, and the information turned over to the proper parties."

"Did you find such wrecks, Captain?"

"I honestly don't know, Ted. The Coast Guard may be able to tell, by correlating its information, but if so, they won't notify me."

Captain Weymouth had something else on his mind, and after searching through his pockets for a moment, drew out a wallet, which he turned over to Ted.

"What do you make of that, Ted? One of the sailors turned it in."

Ted looked it over before opening it. There were only a few dollars inside, and some identification papers. This wallet belonged to someone named Victor Wayne. Victor Wayne! The name rang a sudden bell.

"Do you know who this is, Captain?"

"No, I don't. There's never been a hand on our boat by that name."

"He's a firebug who escaped from prison several months ago. Danny Beach's father has been working on the case."

Captain Weymouth raised his eyebrows. "Then that might explain the fire on our boat, if this Victor Wayne is aboard. I suppose he wouldn't have had much trouble getting aboard while we were moored up the river during the strike."

"Are you going to launch a search for him, Captain?"

"A search? I don't know." Captain Weymouth frowned. If I do it will be a quite private one. I don't want to alert the whole boat. Anyway we've only got two more nights before we reach home, and then we'll watch as the sailors go ashore. I'll put the deck watch on notice, but I don't know that it will help. I doubt very much that we have a stowaway, after all. This Victor Wayne could be a member of our crew under a false name."

This possibility hadn't occurred to Ted, but he saw that it might easily be true. He and Nelson really had no proof of a stowaway on board. But the shortage of money in the wallet bothered him. The three dollar bills were apparently unmarked. A fugitive was likely to be short of money and might want to steal; but this thief was seemingly more interested in stealing money to put into someone else's wallet.

After they were ushered into Commander Lehigh's office, Ted learned that the Coast Guard was returning the captain's favor.

"Have you completed the safety check on the *Shamrock,* Commander?" asked Captain Weymouth, after introductions and pleasantries had been exchanged.

"Yes, Captain, we have. It's all here in this report. We have gone over the plans of the *Shamrock,* and we find her to be a well-designed vessel. There are a number of things that can be improved upon, of course. We think you should have automatic distress-signal transmitters in each of the lifeboats, and your auxiliary electric system is a little faulty. It is tied in too closely with the main system, so that under certain conditions they might both be knocked out. We have outlined a plan for rewiring."

The technical discussion continued for some time—during which Ted was dispatched on several errands—and finally drew to a close with the captain thanking the commander for his fine service.

"I'm sure Mrs. Dundee will appreciate your efforts, too, and will see that your recommendations are acted upon as quickly as possible."

Ted could not help feeling a little let down that the captain's treasure hunt had had such a commonplace explanation. Sometimes, he thought—as in the case of the Lake Superior sea serpent—it was more fun and just as profitable not to know the truth.

As they had anticipated, there was no trouble at all about hiring a motorboat.

"Why, there's the *White Rover,*" Ted exclaimed, without thinking.

"A friend of yours?" asked Captain Weymouth. "Then we might as well hire him as anyone else."

About to object, Ted held his tongue. There was little point in explaining that Captain Blair wasn't exactly a friend, and there was no particular reason why they shouldn't ride with him, if he was willing.

At first not recognizing Ted, Captain Blair realized who he was after he spoke first.

"Oh, one of my friends from Resthaven Cove. What can I do for you?"

Captain Weymouth explained that they were trying to overtake the *Shamrock,* and after ascertaining the time the *Shamrock* had left, Captain Blair promised to reach her before she reached Lake Huron, or not long afterward.

Arrangements were made and they climbed on board. Captain Blair took off, and it was apparent that he was a competent pilot even in the narrow straits and congested waters of the lower St. Marys River. Sitting low in the water gave the illusion of great speed, and the mottled shores sped by. It seemed evident that Captain Blair was going to keep his promise, and would do so without speeding recklessly or taking undue chances.

"Nice craft," Captain Weymouth remarked, and he and Captain Blair exchanged observations about their respective boats.

Ted was satisfied to lean back and relax during the long drive. He spoke only when someone spoke to him, and for the rest enjoyed the passing scenery.

"Had a fishing party up on Lake Superior," Captain Blair called back to him. "I told you I could outfox the lampreys."

"Didn't they want to come back with you?" Ted cried.

"No, we overstayed our time, and they flew back."

Ted's arm rested lightly on the stern as he watched the wake of the twin propellers behind them. Some boats had their names painted on the sides, but the *White Rover's* was on the back. And then it seemed to Ted that something was loose. There was a back panel, he discovered, held in place by screws. The name wasn't painted on the boat itself, but on the panel, which apparently could be removed with very little trouble.

He grew thoughtful. The *Gray Lady,* he believed, had a carrier above the cabin and there was none here. But he saw now that there were brackets on which a carrier could easily be fitted. He found a suppressed excitement swelling up inside him. Could it be that he was riding on the *Gray Lady* this minute?

Still, what was the purpose of it? Why had the *Gray Lady* buzzed the *Shamrock* in harbor, and apparently shadowed them up to Lake Superior until she was scared off by the searchlight? Maybe Captain Blair really did have a fishing party to take up there, and that moonlight adventure was one of his extracurricular—and extralegal—activities. Ted had a feeling that the captain's activities would not bear very careful examination. Perhaps even Captain Xerxes had been right; he had seen the *Gray Lady* coming into Resthaven Cove occasionally in the dead of night, when Captain Blair supposed himself to be unobserved. These retired seamen were more aware than anyone supposed.

When they overtook the *Shamrock,* it hove to, and they moved in amidships. A compartment was opened from which a gangplank could be put out, though Ted had never seen it in operation. But at least it meant a shorter climb aboard. From there they climbed a stairs to the main deck, and watched the *White Rover* speed off down Lake Huron.

He had time to discuss his theory with Nelson, and when he explained why he thought that the *White Rover* and the *Gray Lady* were the same, Nelson whistled.

"Then you think there isn't any mysterious Canadian named Captain Hunt?"

"No, Captain Blair just made up the name for our benefit."

"We thought he refused to show us the *White Rover* right away because he had to make a call warning the *Gray Lady* away. What do you think now?"

"His boat must have been fitted up as the *Gray Lady,* and he needed time to change the name panel and other fittings."

"But even if it's true, it doesn't solve anything, does it?"

"No, I guess not," Ted agreed. "It doesn't tell us whether or not Victor Wayne is a stowaway on this boat," and he startled Nelson with this new information.

He served the officers, and then had supper with Danny. When the latter heard about Victor Wayne's wallet, he was more eager than before to make the evening deck patrol.

Ted grabbed some sleep in the earlier part of the evening. Then he met Nelson coming off duty at midnight, and they debated how long it was worthwhile to search. Their feelings were so mixed on the matter that they contradicted both themselves and each other. Suddenly Ted's attention was caught.

"Nel," he said very quietly, "there *is* somebody hiding between those two hatch covers."

Being careful not to raise his voice or to turn in that direction, Nelson asked Ted just which aisle it was, then suggested:

"Let's get after him!"

"Sure, why not? I'll count three."

At "three" they suddenly dashed off in the direction where Ted was certain he had seen someone. The stowaway, cowering at first, realized that he was discovered and could not hope to hide. He rose and dashed in the opposite direction toward the stairway amidships, then ran down. Ted and Nelson reached the stairs moments later, and clambered down. When they reached the lower deck, there was no one in sight.

"Was it a man or a boy, Ted?"

"I couldn't tell. It might have been a man crouching way over."

They heard a rustle toward the stern.

"After him!" Nelson cried.

They could hear the runner up ahead. He was descending to a lower level. They followed, but without catching sight of him. The *Shamrock* had a double hull, the outer hull and an inner hull which held the ore. Steel girders joined the two shells, and some of the space was partitioned off into rooms and corridors and tanks for oil and ballast, but some of it seemed bare. Here, in a section deep down where they had never been before, the bare girders suggested the framework of a new building.

They heard another noise, a scuffling above the sound of the engine, and turned to follow. They climbed up a ladder, crossed over a tank, and then went down again. The stowaway must have come this way, for there was no other way for him to go. They followed a corridor which took them back to the opposite side of the boat, and climbed a stairs. A door slightly ajar led them into the long curving tunnel which Ted now knew well, dimly lit by intervals of light. As far as they could see the stowaway was not in view. He must have turned back toward the stern of the boat and left the corridor.

Ted and Nelson followed in hot pursuit, only to encounter Mr. Griffith.

"What are you after?" he demanded.

"We're trying to catch someone."

"No one came by me this way."

"Then he must have turned here. After him, Ted!"

They thought they caught sight of a figure turning into the store-room where the food was kept. They followed, and switched on the light. There was no one there.

They had searched this room once before, but now they searched it again, with the same fruitless result. Mr. Griffith had come as far as the doorway, watching them.

"Well, are you satisfied?" he asked, implying he had very little confidence in the stowaway they claimed to have seen.

They should have been satisfied. As far as they could tell there was no other way out of the room, except for the small portholes. A secret panel seemed ridiculous on a boat like the *Shamrock* intended for service without nonsense, and especially unlikely in view of the large cartons stacked in front of most of the wall space.

"Did I hear something?" asked Nelson, detecting a slight movement.

"Possibly a rat," Mr. Griffith suggested.

An authoritative voice behind them spoke up. 'Try the freezer." It was Sam Grant.

"You're crazy, Grant. He'd smother in there."

"All the more reason to check it out pronto."

Nelson opened the door to the freezer. It was well stacked with food, leaving absolutely no room for anyone to hide. There was another freezer set farther back and apparently not in use. Ted flung the door open, revealing a man crouching inside. His quarters were cramped, but he was in no danger of suffocation, for they found that a rear panel had been removed. Hopelessly trapped, the man stepped out.

"It's John Star!" Mr. Griffith exclaimed. "But he wasn't in there when we searched the boat. I'm sure of that."

John Star was taken forward to the captain's quarters by Ted, Nelson, and Mr. Griffith, while Grant returned to his duties. The captain was at first inclined to listen.

"Well, John, what's the explanation of all this?"

The stowaway stared at him, but made no attempt to answer. The captain tried once more.

"Come, come, we'll find out anyway, and it will be better if you tell us all about it."

Still Star did not reply.

"Then I suppose we may assume the worst," the captain said sternly. "Under my authority as captain I place you under arrest. Ted, will you get Custer up here?"

Ted went off, and soon returned with the deck boss.

"We seem to have a stowaway here, Custer. Will you see that this man is kept under lock and key for the rest of the voyage?"

Custer stared. "John Star? I don't like passengers, sir. Why not let me put him to work?"

"No, I'd feel happier with him locked up. He may be a fugitive from justice. How about the carpenter's room?"

"The very place I was thinking of myself."

Ted and Nelson remained behind for a short time to explain how the stowaway was captured. Then they were dismissed.

"Then there really was a stowaway," Nelson remarked, "but it was a man, not a boy. And the reason you thought there was a stowaway was because you felt sure it was a boy starting a fire with that reading glass."

"Well, it was a good theory, wasn't it? It only occurred to me tonight what side of the boat the carpenter's room is on."

"The right side, isn't it?"

"And which side is that when crossing Lake Superior toward Duluth?"

"The north side."

"Then where did he get the sunshine to start a fire?"

Nelson managed a sleepy chortle. "Remember what our logic professor told us? Being right for the wrong reason is the same thing as being wrong. So John Star and Victor Wayne are the same person. How do you like them apples?"

"No, I don't think so, Nel." Nelson looked startled as Ted went on to explain. "Remember the fire. I still don't think it was a serious attempt at arson. And other things don't add up either. By disappearing, John Star drew attention to himself, which is the last thing a fugitive would want to do. And after doing that, he came back on the *Shamrock* again, which is something else Victor Wayne wouldn't have done. And I don't think a real fugitive would be putting money into other people's wallets."

"Well, then, who is Victor Wayne?" Nelson demanded in exasperation. "We're halfway down Lake Huron already. If you've got any brilliant idea coming on, you'd better hurry it up."

"Don't rush me, don't rush me. I'm working on it."

# CHAPTER 15.

## A CONFERENCE AND A CONFRONTATION

A CONFERENCE was arranged to take place at the Coast Guard station, in the office of Commander James Wingate. In attendance, besides Ted and Nelson, were Captain Weymouth, Mrs. Dundee, First Mate Bowling, Chief Engineer Owens, and—surprisingly—Sam Grant.

"There seems to be a need for a meeting of this kind," Commander Wingate began after the visitors were all seated, "to determine as far as we are able just what has been going on aboard the *Shamrock MI*, who has been responsible, what regulations have been violated, and what action is to be taken.

"Merely for the record, I will summarize some of the mishaps. At first there was a series of operational troubles, which may have been due to design or misfortune. Then there were an illicit radio message sending the *Shamrock* to the wrong port, the disappearance of a crew member, a short delay upstream due to a tugboat strike, thefts and other misadventures aboard, and the capture of a stowaway who was the missing crew member.

"John Star is our most immediate concern, since he is in custody and must be charged. Fingerprints have proved that he is not Victor Wayne, whatever else he may have been up to. Since he left the ship and returned he definitely is a stowaway, which is a legal violation, though it may be difficult to prove that he was responsible for many of the mishaps on board. And by disappearing in the manner he did, he put the authorities to a great deal of expense and trouble in conducting an investigation. He faces charges for that. Now Mrs. Dundee?"

The president of Spanner Lines looked around at the circle of faces.

"I expect that Star received a bribe from an official of the Beatrice Lines to instigate enough trouble on the *Shamrock* to endanger its reputation as a reliable carrier. The president of Beatrice Lines is an acquaintance of mine. I shall ask him to look into the matter within his own organization, and if such a bribe was offered, to take appropriate measures. If and when we have proof Star accepted such a bribe, we will decide what to do about it. Now what about Victor Wayne? Do you have an idea about that, Ted?"

"Yes, I've thought a good deal about it, Mrs. Dundee, and the only way I can figure it out is that Victor Wayne was never on board the *Shamrock.* The dropped wallet, and the fire, seem to me designed merely to create his 'presence' on board, after which he would disappear. Such a step would be embarrassing to the officers of the *Shamrock,* and would undoubtedly involve further delays, confusion, and legal red tape, with the possible loss of a vital contract."

"Indeed?" Mrs. Dundee looked very thoughtful. "If Star was masquerading as a known criminal, then he was impeding justice and possibly helping the real criminal to escape. I'm sure that is something else the authorities will want him for. I wish that this closed the matter, but it is obvious that John Star had some help on board in getting off and on the *Shamrock* and in remaining hidden. You had some thoughts about that, too, didn't you, Ted?"

"I have some ideas, but I don't know how good they are," Ted began. "If John Star had simply disappeared, then we might have thought it was for personal reasons. But the fact that he came back on board the *Shamrock* again proved that he had an additional purpose— to create all the dissension and disturbance he could, and blame it on a fugitive Victor Wayne, who would then disappear. Probably he was responsible for the thefts, but when he put my money into someone else's wallet, it's obvious that theft wasn't his real intent. Nor do I think that he could have had any serious intention of setting the *Shamrock* on fire. What good would it do? He might be killed himself, or if rescued, suspicion would certainly rest squarely upon him. I think the same motive guided the person helping him—to cause confusion and delays but nothing desperate that would lead to a very searching investigation.

"It is certain that Star did leave the *Shamrock* and then come back. He left the ship knowing there would be a general search after his disappearance, and returned after the inquiry when he could stow away with little chance of detection. Someone resembling him was seen some weeks ago up in Resthaven Cove, where Captain Blair is stationed. It is my belief that Captain Blair, in a boat masquerading as the *Gray Lady,* tried to smuggle him aboard the night the *Shamrock* lay in harbor, but the attempt went astray. But then the next night the *Shamrock* lay tied up far up the river, and I think this gave a suitable opportunity. The previous attempt was made because it was not certain, at that time, that the tugboat strike would come off and the *Shamrock* be marooned upstream. This is one of the reasons that make me believe the conspirators had no direct connection with the strike, or probably with the flu epidemic, or with several operational accidents which occurred. They were simply ready to jump in and take advantage of every situation which developed.

"If I am correct that it was the *Gray Lady* that tried to smuggle Star on board, it is also probable that the *Gray Lady* was to help him escape in Lake Superior. I imagine that he was supposed to jump overboard with a life jacket, and would probably have some sort of signaling device to guide the *Gray Lady* to him. Unfortunately the moon and the clouds were playing tricks that night, and that scheme went astray.

"As for the person on board helping Star, one man to come under suspicion was Sam Grant, the new wiper. Perhaps you'd like to explain about it yourself, Grant?"

Grant looked embarrassed. "I don't think anything I did was wrong—well, maybe one thing. Anyway, I think Ted has already guessed who I am. My father is William S. Grant, one of the minority stockholders. Mrs. Dundee knows him, and I'm sure she knows that he's not a member of the minority stockholders' group she was expecting trouble with."

"Yes, I'm sure of that," Mrs. Dundee agreed. "You have a fine example before you."

"Well, I graduated from college in June, and came to work in the office. That was all right, but my father always had an idea that if I intended to stay in the company, I should learn the business solidly from the ground up. And I guess everybody knows where the bottom of the pile is—a wiper on a freighter comes pretty close to being it. When the disappearance of John Star left the job open, my father suggested that I take it, and I did. There was only one thing—if my officers learned who I was, and maybe gave me preferential treatment, the whole thing would be useless, and of course I didn't want my fellow workers to know I was the son of a company bigwig, either.

"Oddly enough, there was only one person who might give me away. Mrs. Dundee didn't know me, the officers on the *Shamrock* didn't know me—but one person had met me in the office. That was Danny Beach, at the time he came to the office to sign on the *Shamrock*. I handled that matter for him. Apparently the girl who turned him over to me didn't give my name, or he was too excited to remember it or to remember what I looked like afterward. Of course, we had his telephone number at the office, and I called him to ask him not to give me away, but then when we met on the *Shamrock* it turned out he didn't remember me at all!"

"When he asked you, you denied calling him," Ted reminded him.

"Well, what could I do? It was obvious by then that he didn't know me, and he asked me in front of his friend, with maybe other sailors listening in the background, so what could I say?"

"What about that mistake you made?" said Mr. Owens bluntly. "I'm sure Mr. Griffith never gave you an order like that. Was it ignorance or sabotage?"

"I guess it was just plain ignorance," Grant replied humbly. "I'll say here and now that it wasn't Mr. Griffith's fault. I've had some experience around cars, so I thought I knew what I was doing, but I found out a steam engine is something different. They don't even use the same terms. It wasn't Mr. Griffiith's fault that I pretended to know a lot more than I did—but that's something I'll never do again."

Ted smiled and resumed his explanation: "Another person who came under suspicion was Lynn Kilbane, the radio man. I'm sure it must have occurred to a great many people that he could have faked that message himself. As far as I am concerned he cleared himself when I caught him putting back the money that had been stolen from my wallet. Of course, you could say that he just had an attack of conscience and wanted to make things good again, but if he was in league with the conspirators, he had a lot more on his conscience than twenty dollars.

"So it's my opinion that Kilbane really received that message, and if he did, where did it come from? The company office was a likely explanation, since it had to come from somebody who knew a good deal about operating methods. But it didn't have to be the company, either, if the person sending it was closely in touch with things aboard the *Shamrock.* I can think of another explanation that's attractive. That message could have originated from another boat, let's say the *Gray Lady,* which may have been not too far off from the *Shamrock.*

"At least we know that the *White Rover* could have been in the vicinity each time the *Gray Lady* was sighted. Do you suppose, Commander Wingate, you could check on whether the *White Rover* has a radio transmitter aboard?"

"Why, yes, Ted, that's very easily done." He reached to a shelf for a register, and leafed through it. "There's no record here that Captain Blair's boat is licensed for radio transmission."

Ted felt a little discouraged. Of course, this didn't necessarily prove that Captain Blair couldn't have sent the message; and even if he did have a radio, it wouldn't prove that he did. Still, it was a small but suggestive point. Then suddenly a more exciting idea occurred to him which seemed even more likely.

"What about Captain Joseph Hunt, owner of a boat called the *Gray Lady?* He would be a Canadian."

The commander reached for another register, and looked through it. "Yes, Captain Hunt does have a radio transmitter on board, but that still would be no proof that he sent the message."

And still no one caught on to Ted's idea. Well, he could be wrong, and he hated to be wrong in front of so many important people, but his hunch was strong, and he decided to go for broke.

"What about Captain Hunt? Can you give me any information about his appearance, and so on?"

"It's not in this book, but if you think it worthwhile I can radio the Canadian authorities." Ted nodded, and the commander left the room. The group sat quietly, tensely, until he returned a few minutes later. "Yes, they had a physical description of him: about forty years old, five foot ten, weight almost two hundred pounds, sandy hair—well?"

Now Nelson had caught on, and sat bolt upright. "Why, that's a description of Captain Blair!"

"I think so myself," said Ted. "Captain Blair and Captain Hunt are the same person, and the *White Rover* and the *Gray Lady* are the same boat."

"You still haven't proved that the message came from Captain Blair," Captain Weymouth pointed out.

"Nevertheless," said Commander Wingate, "if Captain Blair secured a Canadian transmitting license by giving a false name to the authorities, I think they are going to be very much interested in hearing about it. I think we can safely leave Captain Blair to the tender mercies of our Canadian friends." He shot a glance of admiration toward Mrs. Dundee and Captain Weymouth. "Anything else, Ted?"

"We still haven't touched upon the way John Star disappeared. Something kind of strange happened one day when I was on shore. I got to talking with an old fisherman, and he was just about to tell us an interesting story when we were interrupted by a fire in a rowboat, so we never did get to hear his story. And I don't think even he realized how important his story was, because he left town that day, before word of the disappearing sailor reached the newspapers.

"I was thinking of that when we turned into the harbor yesterday, and I suddenly realized what could have happened. I don't think Star swam to shore, and I don't think he was picked up by a boat. But there was another way to get to shore, and I realized it when I heard the whistling buoys on that old-fashioned water crib four or five miles out in the lake."

His listeners looked amazed, and Ted went on quickly, "I called the water department to see if anyone was working out on the crib that evening, and no one was—the conspirators could easily have found that out. Star probably jumped from the dark side of the boat where he could not be visible from shore. A small figure like that swimming through the water would not be noticeable either. And it was hoped that he wouldn't be seen scrambling up to the crib, but here they were mistaken. I believe he *was* seen by my fisherman friend, who assumed it to be a simple mishap at sea, and didn't think it necessary to report the matter as long as the sailor was safe. How Star got to shore is uncertain. I don't think the *Gray Lady* would have dared pick him up, but Captain Blair may have hidden a rowboat at the crib in advance, and Star used it to row ashore, or there may have been a spare boat there."

Ted paused and looked around. He was getting close attention, mixed with a little skepticism until his listeners had a chance to work the whole thing out in their own minds.

"I think there is just one more thing. Lynn Kilbane told me that a pamphlet from Beatrice Lines was hidden among his things, but I think he is mistaken. I think that he accidentally picked it up on the bridge, and that this was as embarrassing to someone else as it was to him. We know that John Star had help from someone on the *Shamrock*. It would probably have been someone with access to the radio, in order to send some sort of cryptic message to the *Gray Lady* that everything was ready and to proceed with the plan. It would have to be somebody who wouldn't question the message when it came in, and would make sure that the *Shamrock* sailed close enough to the crib so that John Star could swim to it." Ted looked straight at the first mate. "And that was you."

Kirt Bowling sprang to his feet, his face furious. "You're loony. I wasn't even supposed to be on the bridge that night."

"I know, but the second mate had a convenient headache, and needed very little persuasion to let you stand his trick. I feel sure that if it hadn't been for that lucky chance, you would have found some other method of persuading him to change shifts with you."

Then Bowling turned to Captain Weymouth. "Do I have to stand here and listen to twaddle coming from a fugitive from a nursery school?"

"Why, no," said the captain. "I'm sure that all of us will be willing to listen to anything you have to say."

The first mate looked around at the hostile faces. "You realize that I can't continue on the *Shamrock* when you allow accusations like that to be made in my presence."

"Your resignation is accepted," said Captain Weymouth. He seemed to be taking things calmly, either through long experience or because he had never quite had the fullest confidence in his first mate. But Mrs. Dundee and Mr. Owens both looked shocked.

Bowling spun about and cast one more glance of hatred at Ted, before saying, "You'll be hearing from my lawyer about this," and banged out of the room.

And now Ted, looking around, could see that all doubt had disappeared. But no one was feeling very elated over the turn matters had taken.

"I suppose Beatrice Lines made him a good offer," said Captain Weymouth, soberly. "More than likely he was promised a captaincy. Too bad. He would have made a good captain, except—well, the sea is always sincere, and I guess the only way we can successfully meet it is with our own sincerity."

"What's going to happen now?" asked Nelson. "Will he sue?"

"On what grounds?" said Mrs. Dundee, her voice, too, sounding weary with disappointment. "If you are asking what I intend to do, I'll have to consult my own lawyer about that. But his career is ruined. What worse punishment could a man have?

"I think you've done everything I could have hoped for, and far, far more than I expected. Money could never express my gratitude, but would you be insulted if I should try?"

"We're pretty hard to insult," said Nelson happily, before Ted could speak, and Ted, about to object, changed his mind and smiled instead.

As they walked in a group away from the Coast Guard station, Ted said to the captain:

"There's one thing I don't understand that for a time made me suspect Mr. Keats. When I served my trick on the bridge coming up on Lake Huron, I sighted a freighter, and yet the bridge refused to report it. Can you explain that to me?"

"Yes, Ted, it happens I can. You did not see a freighter that morning."

"But Captain—" Ted protested.

"What you saw, Ted, was a mirage. I know, because the bridge reported on it to me later. Didn't it seem to disappear too quickly?"

"Well, yes," Ted admitted.

"It's hard for a novice to believe it, the first time he sees a clear mirage, and even old hands are occasionally taken in. But the phenomenon is quite common on the Lakes, and undoubtedly contributes to the stories about phantom boats. I imagine that there *was* a freighter, far beyond the horizon, and that the image was reflected to you due to peculiar atmospheric conditions. Very often the mirage will take the form of a boat riding upside down in the sky, in which case it will be apparent that your eyes are playing tricks on you. Sometimes there will be a double image, the upside-down boat in the sky and a rightside-up boat on the water. It's my guess that you saw the lower half of a double image."

"If I'd only had a picture of that," said Nelson sadly. "My trouble is I don't get up early enough in the morning."

When all farewells and thanks had been said, Nelson and Ted stood for a moment looking out at the harbor, and what might be their last view of the *Shamrock*.

"I guess *My Shamrock* will be sailing soon," Ted said, "and without us this time."

"You know something, Ted? That's the first time I ever heard you call her *'My' Shamrock*. But she was sort of getting to seem like home. A lot of good things happened there, and a few bad things, too."

"Just like home," said Ted.

www.ingramcontent.com/pod-product-compliance
Lightning Source LLC
Chambersburg PA
CBHW020656180626
46816CB00003B/1319